WORDS
INTO
WISHES

An eclectic mix of short stories
and flash fiction – compiled for
the **Children with Cancer Fund**

Copyright ©Scribe Tribe

Names, characters, places and incidents are products of the author's imagination or are used fictitiously. Any resemblance to actual persons living or dead is entirely co-incidental.

Acknowledgement

We would like to thank Drew and the staff at Bibendum in Eastbourne for giving us use of a room for our meetings. They look after us very well and show interest in what we do.

FOREWORD

CWCF was formed in July 1998 and is made up of a small office team and local volunteers, with the main thought being to enable the children, and families of the children with cancer, to have a quality of life that we would hope to have ourselves.

Although it doesn't sound professional (so I've been told), the four of us were sat round a pub table, out for a drink and wanted to 'have our own baby' within the community. I consider myself lucky to be doing what we are and to be able to have a little input to the lives of the families going through cancer locally.

Chris Downton, Founder

Children with Cancer Fund
4, the Triangle
Willingdon
Eastbourne
BN20 9 PJ
Registered Charity No. 1110644

www.childrenwithcancerfund.org.uk

INTRODUCTION

Welcome to this collection of short stories from the Scribe Tribe writing group in Eastbourne.

These have been written during different phases, different moods and this is reflected in their range, covering a wide spectrum of emotions. Our group meets weekly and decided it would be a worthwhile exercise to do something useful with our prolific output.

You have already read Chris's foreword so can see that the local charity 'The Children with Cancer Fund' would be a worthy cause for money raised by selling our book.

Hopefully you will enjoy reading our stories that are often inspired by a random selection of words we all contribute. By buying the book you are helping turn our Words into Wishes for the children.

(Available from Amazon and via the Children with Cancer website)

CONTENTS

THE ROAD	1
MY BROTHER	6
THIS BOY	8
SHADOWS	11
BUBBLES	16
THE ANONYMOUS MUSICIAN'S JOURNEY	19
THE MISSING LINK	22
VANESSA'S INDULGENCE	26
THE HERB GARDEN	29
WAR TOY STORY	32
THE WITCHY WOMAN	33
MEMORIES OF MANDY	40
PSYCHIC	42
FREEDOM	45
DANUBE DELTA DRAMA	48
BEHIND CLOSED DOORS	55
THE LOTTERY	58
THE HOLIDAY	60
TRAPPED	64
RECYCLING	67

NEW START	75
A PERFECT PLACE TO HIDE	79
THE LAST PHONEBOX IN LONDON	88
THE POLICEMAN	93
DAN	96
FORGETFUL	99
LIVE AND LET LIVE	102
THE DESERT	107
RISING HIGH	110

THE ROAD

Step out of Eastbourne's Victorian railway station, and you are transported in time. Not a bygone romantic time that old sepia-toned postcards give you, but the future. Stand there a while and take in the panoramic view. Let your eyes adjust to the intensity of light - a light that only seaside resorts give. The view could be any such image of any town, but now breathe in. The smell is different, distinct, and separate from similar places. It suggests purity, invigoration, and new beginnings. These senses are all due to one thing, the smell of the sea – brine. You won't need your satnav. The road you are on is the one you need to follow to the sea.

Like every other town there is the sense of Clonesville – convenience stores, take-a-ways, 'To Let' signs in unwashed, cracked windows, the growth of charity shops. But wait, a ray of sunshine emerges. A converted Victorian Bank - clean, shiny, bright, with gold and red signs of warmth and comfort. Nearby a Wetherspoons, saviours of town centres, where all are welcome. The Road ahead used to be tree lined with upmarket shops. Nazi bombs got rid of the posh shops and forced rebuilding of cheap concrete ugly ones in the 1950s. Trees have gone more recently, health and safety rules and council cuts, saw to that. The Road though, is still there, permanent as ever, moving with constant streams of people going who knows where. New brick block paving feels solid underfoot and looks cleaner and smarter than old tarmac while flowerbeds in the centre soften the scheme. A new shopping centre, The Beacon, enjoyed by many with cinema and restaurants has all weather appeal.

The Road cuts through the heart of the town, splitting it neatly in two, both economically and politically, making it the hub. That may be temporal, but the Road, like its foundation, is solid and just keeps on going to the sea. The Road has stories of its own to tell.

On the left is where Leapy Lee performed regularly in the 1960s. The Panorama coffee bar was the must be place, for all teenage rock-n-rollers to meet one another. Now a forlorn charity shop occupies the spot. Opposite McDonald's marks an alleyway, leading to where Jack's late-night cafe, offered tea and fry ups to regulars on tick. Jack also had a sideline, for which he spent years at her majesty's pleasure, for performing back street abortions in exchange for favours.

Continuing along the Road is Bankers Corner, the real hub of the town, where all social classes congregate regularly. Carrying on through what were elegant Regency houses this is now a pedestrian precinct. On the right-hand side of the precinct is a rather beautiful huge circular window above a shop. Worth more than a glance. It was here in 1960 that Sabrina, the sex goddess of the time, opened the town's first Tesco store.

The seaside atmosphere builds as gulls swoop and squawk, and coffee shop aromas try to tempt you in. A young busker strums Cavatina, competing with the lonely man stopping passers-by and trying to sell them God. Some stop to enjoy the music, before The Road brings the visitor to another entrance of the shopping centre. This was once the entrance to The Continental where dreams were made and dashed and couples met. Often referred to as 'the stairway to heaven' this coffee bar was the main hangout for the Mods and Rockers alike in the 1960s. Outside scooters and motorbikes were parked side by side, nightly, while their teenage owners were upstairs, dancing, and drinking espresso coffees. A little further along is the 1950s Marks & Spencer store. Its 1920s predecessor got a direct Nazi hit in 1941 killing dozens of shoppers and staff, mainly women and girls.

A short detour to the left, to All Souls Church, is worthwhile. Visitors are greeted by an amazing mock Byzantine church and tower. Its red and white brickwork are truly impressive. Even more spectacular is the beautiful interior glazed tile work and furniture. Visitors will not have been disappointed with this enriching and therapeutic visit reinvigorating them for the journey ahead. Retracing one's footsteps and continuing seawards, brings you to the town's biggest store Debenhams – now closed. Windows are decorated with artwork aiming to look cheerful and plans of new retail developments with housing above sound promising. These things take time…

Continuing and following the strengthening pull of the Channel, are more charity shops. At the next junction are two grand buildings of Eastbourne's opulent past - TJ Hughes, now closed - and the defunct 1920s Coop now a charity shop and Travelodge.

At this junction another short diversion is worthwhile. Turn right to be greeted by the beautiful Holy Trinity church, designed by Decimus Burton in 1839. Further along on the right is Kent House, once the surgery of Bodkin Adams. Eastbourne's most notorious doctor, he was the recipient of wealthy women's fortunes, after allegedly helping them to their untimely and unwanted end. He was charged with multiple murders, but the case was abandoned due to a technicality of law.

Retracing one's steps back to the Road will bring the visitor to the final part of the journey to the sea. This part of Terminus Road is along what was considered in the 1920s Eastbourne's most elegant shopping parade, called Victoria Place, now mostly restaurants, cafes, ice cream parlours, with a smattering of antique and charity shops. Outside seating and musical entertainment in summer cafe enhance the culture now prevalent. The smell and intensity of the sea is noticeable now as one continues past a myriad of ethnic food establishments, a traditional sweet shop, and seaside souvenirs, before reaching the Burlington Hotel. Ahead is the sea where a long pause is recommended. Look East and be greeted by the wow factor – the famous Carpet Gardens, backdropped by the 19th century Pier standing beautiful, proud and solid.

To the West lie the Art Deco Bandstand and Napoleonic Wish Tower. Striking and elegant, these structures are both dominated by nearby Beachy Head which is famous for its spectacular scenery and lighthouse but infamous for its tragic suicides.

You have just travelled an amazing journey along a Road which slices through Eastbourne's heart, dividing its population, politically and economically but also uniting its citizens in shopping, eating, entertainment, hanging around or just walking towards the sea.

Denis MacReever

MY BROTHER

There are nasty people, selfish people and plain, simple stupid people, and my brother Charlie has been all three over the years. Never a thought for other people, always wrapped up in himself. He liked things a certain way, and normally got what he wanted. It was his way or no way as they say. It never ceased to amaze me. In fact, I found it quite abhorrent.

Especially, when he was nasty. People like that can't normally see any further than their nose. Still, he made me laugh at times but karma does have a way of catching up. As it did for Charlie who still lives on his own.

Talk about windy weather and always changing directions. He didn't know what way his ship was sailing half the time. No wonder he found it hard to keep a partner. He was far too selfish at the end of the day.

I can't tell you how many times he was let down by women over the years. And I can't say I blamed them. Charlie was hard work and as his only sister, I could certainly tell you a story or two.

He wasn't bad looking in his younger years as it goes and could pull most women with his chat alone. Mind you, it was embarrassing once, when he took me and this really flamboyant woman out to a musical. Her name was Lorretta and she was tall, with long curly hair and big bosoms. She had teeth that went ping when she smiled as well. Charlie thought he was in with a chance and was trying to impress her. He thought she'd be putty in his hand. But she turned out to be quite pompous.

He'd tossed a coin as to whether he or his friend would date her too. Half way through the show though, she got up and scarpered, saying, 'this wasn't a show for ladies.' Still, given Charlie's reputation, she was either very smart or asinine. I'd go for the latter, only I saw her a week later with a guy I knew from school. He was hardly brains of Britain and I heard he went out with anyone that moved.

Years later, I learnt a little more about Lorretta. And as it happened, she wasn't such a lady at all. The real reason she walked out on Charlie was because half the cast knew her. Or should I say, him. Only Lorretta normally played the part of Dame, during their Christmas production. Full rig out and make up to boot. Just as she looked when she went out with my brother.

Now there's nothing wrong with that except my brother didn't know the full details. After all he would have had a shock if he'd taken her back to his place, which was his intention, can you imagine.

I think Charlie had a lucky escape. Or as it goes, perhaps he did like things a certain way. Who knows, he is still single.

Lena Bowling

THIS BOY

I think it's about time that I told the world who I am. I have had so many labels that it made me laugh, but now it's getting annoying. Mostly I have behaviour problems, (school,) called weird, (fellow pupils,) simple, (trades people,) annoying, (my father,) waste of space, (my mother,) and now sociopath (probation officer.) On social media and the News more simply *That Boy*!

Due to all these people around me I decided to research my own condition. To my delight I have self-diagnosed myself to be neuro diverse. Wow! That makes sense! I am thrilled. Apparently so is Einstein. Genius! An intrinsic diversity in human brain function and cognition.

This make it very difficult to have to relate to stupid people, who I have been plagued with all my life. I don't really like people anyway; I don't understand their ridiculous responses. They are just not logical, full of inappropriate emotional content that has no bearing on the reality of life.

I used to like my maths teacher, at least he made sense for a while, but then I sort of outgrew him. I don't go to school anymore anyway. That can be problematic, as I am 14, but I have sorted out a way round it. I go out in my uniform, attend registration, and then disappear to a library, I think they do know but turn a blind eye. They are tired and it is easier, and it suits me too. I choose different libraries each time, which is proving expensive taking trains and buses. This has caused my current difficulty to which I have yet to detect a solution.

I actually think libraries are heaven on earth. Ha ha, as if there is a heaven, honestly! They are literally the only places I can find peace. I can anaesthetise myself completely in my beloved maths, where everything makes sense. If I had to have a religion, it would be pure maths. I assess I am post graduate stage now and would dearly love to do a PhD but that will take a bit of organising. I may have to wait a while due to my current situation.

It is so expensive you see. Research at this level is, I have to buy books as well as an expensive computer, travel expenses and I do need to eat. I've also had to buy speed from a dealer to enable me to keep energised and Ritalin to help my concentration. All of this doesn't come cheap.

I naturally found a solution. We live next door to a typically waste of space individual. He is supposed to be disabled but looks perfectly ok to me. Disabled with stupidity I would think. He is always moaning on about not having any money and being on benefit. Well, what does he expect? He lives in the pub and smokes about sixty cigarettes a day. Well, add that up. I have been raiding his house and a few others for years. They are usually out at work all day don't seem to have a clue about security. Windows open etc. Honestly, stupid, how these people get jobs I can't think.

Anyway, very recently, I went into my neighbour's house, thinking he was down the pub, but of course he wasn't. there was a tiny bit of an argument, nothing much, and he got angry and pushed me. Well naturally we all have a right to defend ourselves and I pushed him back. Due to his weight problem, (greed and ignorance) he fell hard and hit his head on the fireplace and was out like a light. Apparently, he died but guess who got the blame!

Now I am in a police cell, trying to work out how I can avoid prison. I am sure I will manage it. Juries are randomly selected from the general population. Fifty percent female (hormonal) fifty percent men (alcoholics or TV dulled morons.) It's basic maths: one hundred per cent thick. My chance to shine!

Jane Kenton-Wright

SHADOWS

Excerpts from the Journal of Eliza June Monroe born 16th May 1920

30th November 1941

Nothing really of note. Of course, there is much talk of the war in Europe and whether Mr Churchill will succeed in getting us in, especially since the Rueben was sunk by the Germans. Hope not, I don't want Joe to have to go to fight and there is enough going on here anyway. Another earthquake in Los Angeles. Glad we don't live there. Don't get earthquakes in New England. Do get the cold though. Thanksgiving was cold and wet but we have lots to be thankful for in our little corner here.

One strange thing has been happening that I can't explain and no one else seems to see. Not mom and dad, Harry, or any of my friends. But I see it everywhere. It's like a shadow, a smoke like cloud over everything. Even on a bright day - when we get them - a dark cloak dims the sun. I feel I am constantly in shade. It is menacing - telling me that something terrible is coming. I have tried to explain to Joe but even he, who loves me, thinks I am a little crazy. Maybe I am but this shadow, shade, gray cloak or whatever, is real to me and something will happen - something big and monumental. Maybe to do with the war. Whatever it is with each passing day the shadow grows longer and darker. The terrible event edges closer and closer.

7th December

I awoke this morning to the darkest shadow I have yet experienced. The room was charcoal; the air was heavy like it was weighing down on me. I knew today would be the day; today the shadow would reveal the event it foretold. And so it did. I was right. We listened to the radio in astonishment and shock. My family did not link the event with my premonition of doom. Why would they? Just my imagination. But I knew and once the announcement had been made the shadow disappeared, I could see bright light again.

Of course, for many including my dear Joe, their road would be a sort of shadow lasting for how long? Hopefully not too long. December 7th 1941 – the day the Japanese bombed Pearl Harbor. The sky was full of dark clouds of smoke and Mr Churchill had us in the war at last.

Journal of Eliza June Carson, nee Monroe

May 16th 1980

So, I have a granddaughter, Ashley; born healthy at 5 and on my own birthday no less. Max and Alice are overjoyed. My one and only child has provided Joe and I with, hopefully, the first of many. She is, of course, quite perfect and appears to favor me so they say. Obviously, I am very happy but there is one cloud over this joyous occasion and it is something that has happened once before, long ago. The shadow that enveloped me just before Pearl Harbor has returned. What does it foretell now, if anything? Much has happened in the last 39 years. Many awful things have affected our country including the Kennedy assassinations and the war in Vietnam which thank God Max survived but the shadow did not touch me. Why now? Only time will tell. Back to some more pleasant matters. Joe and I must introduce ourselves to our new granddaughter.

May 18th 1980

A terrible thing happened today. The same even darker shadow was with me when I woke just as it was back then. As then I heard about the event on the radio. It was the largest ever eruption of a volcano here. Mount St Helens in Washington State had been active for a couple of months but this was the big one. The scenes on TV are apocalyptic. The cloud, the gray ash cloud, made my shadow real again just as the smoke from the destruction of Pearl Harbor made it real then. Whether there are any deaths or will be isn't known yet but my own darkness has lifted now so I will turn away from shadows and instead bathe in the delight of Ashley.

**Excerpts of the Journal of Ashley Carson
born 16th May 1980**

1st September 2001

Went to visit Grandma Eliza today. I have always been able to talk to her, tell her stuff I couldn't possibly tell mom. She is one sweet lady my grandma, she always seems to understand. Things were so different for her when she was 21, waiting all through the war for Grandpa Joe to come back. She's on her own now and still misses him so I hope my visits cheer her up, dear old thing.

    She's told me lots of stories and that's why I could share an odd one of mine. I knew she would listen and not judge me. I had to tell her – how it came upon me suddenly and is growing darker and heavier. That is how she explained it to me, how she explained her shadows. She reassured me I was not going crazy. I did tell mom and dad but they couldn't grasp what I was saying.

    Grandma told me the last time it happened to her was a couple of days after I was born and having seen footage of both Mount St Helens and Pearl Harbor her experiences and the events they relate to are so much like mine. Are we psychic? Is it because we share a birthday? I didn't think psychics were for real - fooling gullible people for money - but now I'm not so sure. This feeling, feeling of being wrapped around with a gray shroud of deep shadows is real. What is coming? What event with black smoke and clouds of gray is coming? Grandma tried to be upbeat but we both know something very bad is going to happen very soon. Perhaps this gift, curse, passes down the female line – who can say? Whatever is coming, it is on an unimaginable scale and it is a certainty.

September 11th

The planes, two, exploding into the buildings, the clouds of thick smoke, the ash and dust raining down from the sky as the huge towers collapsed. My cloud, my smoke, my shadows made real. No more Twin Towers. Please no more shadows ever again. No more words.

Jackie Harvey

BUBBLES

Bill knew it was a mistake. His friend Joe had told him - if you get a dog your benefits will go up.

Bill had been homeless for nearly ten years but managed quite well. He was a Veteran from the conflict in Afghanistan and suffered from P.T.S.D after seeing some good mates get killed. He couldn't bear feeling enclosed, so he slept in a shelter on the seafront.

The Salvation Army would give him free meals and provide hot showers when needed but this dog was driving him mad. Apparently, it was a cockapoo and the previous owner found it too much work. It was a waste of twenty valuable pounds. The damn dog wouldn't stop barking - every seagull or passer-by set him off.

It was late, and no-one was around. Why was the dog still barking? Over the roar of the sea, he could hear someone crunching over the shingle. With some trepidation he walked onto the promenade and, peering into the gloom, saw a shadow by the water's edge. The shadow waded into the sea and disappeared. Bill hesitated, then ran down the steps to the sea. The shadow, a woman, bobbed up gasping. He waded in and grabbed one of her hands. The waves battered them both as if trying to drag her back. Eventually they collapsed onto the shingle both exhausted.

'What the hell were you doing?'

'I wanted to end it all,' the woman sobbed.

'Don't you dare,' Bill yelled, his voice full of emotion - 'life's too precious.' They were both shivering by now.

'I'm sorry, I'm sorry.' She wept.

'Ok Let's get you home. Where do you live? '

She told him she had a flat near the seafront. Bill grabbed the dog and they headed back to her flat. She opened the door; Bill stood there dripping.

'Please come in I'll get you some towels and some of my husband's clothes.' She went into the bedroom and returned with a bundle. 'The bathroom's just down the hall.'

In the bathroom Bill stripped off his wet clothes, had a wash to warm himself, dried off and got dressed. The clothes were a bit loose but felt warm. He walked into the living room; the woman was sitting on the couch wearing a dressing gown with a towel round her head. The dog was snuggled up next to her.

'He likes you.'

She smiled. 'What's his name?'

Bill paused. 'Er, Dog.'

'You can't call him Dog' she exclaimed. 'You should call him Bubbles.'

Bill frowned.

'Oh, there's a cup of tea for you.'

Looking at her Bill could hardly believe what had happened an hour ago.

'What were you thinking?' He said.

'I lost my husband suddenly last year,' she said tearfully. 'We moved by the seaside when he retired but a heart attack took him. I feel so lonely!' She began crying again.

They talked for a little longer, then Bill said he needed to go.

'Do you have a black bag for my clothes?'

'Leave them here I'll wash and dry them for you.'

'Can you look after the dog tonight?'

'Yes of course and thank you.' She smiled.

'You can bring him back tomorrow; you know where I am.'

The next morning, the woman bought Bill a coffee and returned his laundered clothes. The dog was its usual yappy self. He could see the woman liked the dog.

'You take him,' said Bill. 'Dogs are a great way to meet people.'

The woman smiled gratefully.

David Smith

THE ANONYMOUS MUSICIAN'S JOURNEY

In a village nestled among rolling hills and whispering trees, there lived a man known only as the Anonymous Musician. He wandered the cobblestone streets, his guitar slung over his shoulder, weaving melodies that danced through the air like leaves caught in a gentle breeze.

The villagers marvelled at his talent, yet none knew his true name or origins. Some whispered rumours of a troubled past, while others speculated, he was simply a wandering minstrel seeking solace in his songs.

One crisp autumn afternoon, as the leaves painted the ground with hues of gold and amber, the Anonymous Musician sat beneath a towering oak tree, strumming his guitar with a soulful rhythm. A constable passing by paused to listen, his footsteps falling silent as the music enveloped him.

'Beautiful,' the constable remarked, tipping his hat. 'You sustain the spirit of this village with your melodies.'

The musician smiled gratefully, adjusting his glasses before plucking the strings once more. Music has a way of bringing us together, even in the darkest of times.

As the day waned and the sky painted itself with strokes of orange and pink, the constable bid farewell and continued his rounds. The musician remained beneath the oak tree, the fading sunlight casting long shadows over the twigs and fallen leaves scattered at his feet.

Perhaps it was the magic of the music or the tranquil beauty of the setting, but something stirred within him that evening. With a sense of purpose, he resolved to share his gift beyond the borders of his village.

With his guitar strapped securely to his back and a sense of anticipation in his heart, the Anonymous Musician embarked on a journey, his destination unknown, guided only by the whispers of the wind and the beat of his own rhythm.

Through lush valleys and over mist-covered mountains, he travelled, his music echoing through the forests and across the plains. Along the way, he encountered strangers who became friends, their faces illuminated by the warmth of his melodies.

Under starlit skies and beneath billowing clouds the musician found solace in the simplicity of each moment, his mobile existence anchored by the universal language of music.

As the seasons turned and the years passed, tales of the Anonymous Musician spread far and wide, his name whispered in awe by those who had been touched by his music. Yet, despite his newfound fame, he remained humble, a solitary figure wandering the winding roads of the world.

And so, the legend of the Anonymous Musician endured, his songs weaving through the fabric of time like a thread connecting hearts and souls across the ages. Although his true identity remained a mystery, his music spoke volumes, a testament to the power of harmony and the beauty of the human spirit.

Tina Burnett-Evans

THE MISSING LINK

The queue at Primark was long but Stella was happy to wait as, since she had lost over 12lbs, she was eager to buy some skinny clothes to show off her new figure. Suddenly a woman made her way towards Stella. The lady handed her an envelope then disappeared amongst the crowd. The envelope was addressed to Stella.

Diane, her partner in crime on this shopping spree, looked quizzically at her. They were both surprised at this strange happening. Then the queue began to move forward. The envelope was stuffed into her bag to be investigated later on. They moved another two paces forward. Stella was so keen to get in and find the leggings and tops that were on her list.

At home after an exhausting day of shopping, the bags bulged.

'I certainly did not mean to blow the remainder of my monthly allowance but there were so many great clothes. Nine days to go until the end of the month so no more shopping until then.'
She shared with Diane.
Diane had just as many large paper carriers.

'What do you think of this co-ordination – brown and orange, isn't it vibrant?' Diane asked, posing before the mirror like a mannequin.

'I prefer the blues and greens, couldn't decide so bought them both.' replied Stella.

They shared a pizza before Diane went off to the guest room and collapsed into bed. Stella's Mum and Dad had gone away for the weekend, knowing that Diane would keep their daughter company and they could manage on their own.

Stella hung up and put away all her new hoard, then she remembered the envelope. It was in her handbag downstairs. She found her handbag then unzipped the pocket to find the envelope.

It was quite bulky, but as she was not sure what it contained, she felt a little scared to open it. What if it had some poisonous powder inside? She had heard about such things on the TV.

On the other hand, she was sure she had not upset anyone or said anything hurtful for a person to wish to get rid of her. 'Perhaps I will wait until the morning.' She voiced her decision. Leaving the puzzle on the table she went up to her room.

The nightly toothbrushing completed, and eye make-up removed, Stella curled up under the blankets but could not sleep. The envelope, why? What was inside? her brain went round and round. Who was that woman? Stella was sure she had seen her about town or perhaps walking past her house.

More tossing and turning, eventually she put on the light, got out of bed, grabbed her gown and ran down the stairs hurriedly wrapping the belt around her now much smaller waist. She found the envelope which she had left on the table in the lounge. The thought came to her, she would put on a pair of rubber gloves, get a knife, slit it open over a piece of newspaper and see if any powder or poison fell out.

Stella took a deep breath and eased the blade along the sealed edge. No powder, nothing. Gingerly she squashed the corners to spread the two sides. She peered in. A plastic bag with a lock of hair was visible. There was also a folded sheet of paper.

She read:

'Please forgive me for not communicating with you sooner. I was assured you were brought up in a loving home and are growing into a beautiful young lady. Please do not be angry but the truth needs to be told.

My sister became involved in an affair with a married man resulting in a pregnancy that could not bring the joy it should have. Circumstances were difficult and the baby girl was adopted.

You are that darling baby.

As you approach adulthood and spread your wings you have the right to know about your birth mother. She was heartbroken and could never forgive herself for what she had been forced to do. This led to her committing suicide some years ago. I have enclosed a photograph of my sad but sweet sister. Her name was Irene.

Over the last thirteen years I have wanted to communicate with you but kept hesitating in case the whole situation would upset you.

The decision was taken out of my hands when my terminal diagnosis was confirmed. So, I have written this letter to you enclosing a lock of my hair, so that you can delve into your history with the aid of DNA tests.

The best of wishes for a wonderful future of which unhappily, I cannot be a part.

Your uncle, Jeff.'

Gladys Lopato

VANESSA'S INDULGENCE

Vanessa gave a sigh of relief as she heard the front door close. Or rather bang shut, as her husband left to go to his football match. Now was her time – the only break she had in the week from Leonard's *poor me* routine, threats of committing suicide and constant criticising. Nothing pleased him; it was exhausting. Originally, she did sympathise with him – how could she not, when he had lost a leg in the Falklands War. But that was years ago. He made little or no attempt to take advantage of help for injured soldiers from either miliary establishments or the NHS and eventually her sympathy, along with their friends who no longer called, turned to loathing.

She had always loved nice things but with his stinginess – another of the traits she hated – he never gave her enough money to run the house let alone buy anything he considered unnecessary. Every item they owned was either second hand or dirt cheap.

Determined to beat his meanness bit by bit over the years she managed to secrete enough money away to buy a very expensive Wedgewood teapot along with the cream jug and two cups with saucers. Her next purchase would be two tea plates and eventually a larger plate for serving biscuits. She didn't have enough money for these items yet.

When she was sure he wasn't coming back on some pretext or other she went to her secret hiding place and retrieved her precious china. She put her lace table cloth on the coffee table and made herself a pot of Darjeeling tea. She then poured the milk in her cup and the one opposite for her pretend guest then sat back wallowing in the sheer indulgence of her actions. Then she heard the front door open. Help! What could she do? There wasn't time to clear the table.

'The match was cancelled – three players had Covid.' He shouted from the hall then opened the living room door. 'What the hell is going on here? Where did you get all that stuff?'

Without giving her a chance to answer he swiped the teapot and cups on the floor smashing them to pieces and spilling the hot tea everywhere.

'How dare you! The only decent possessions I have in my life and you've broken them.' She bellowed.

He went to hit her; lost his balance and fell onto the shards of china. He yelled, tried to get up then slipped on the wet floor and landed on his side. Quick as a flash Vanessa jumped on him, pushed his neck onto a particularly lethal looking piece of china and held it there hoping she has judged the correct position of the jugular vein. She had. His blood mixed with tea on the floor into a colourful pool. Eventually he stopped thrashing about and was silent. She got to her feet amazed at the strength you can summon up when its needed. Realisation of what she had done suddenly hit her. Oh my god, I've killed him, did I mean to? She asked herself. Do I care that he's dead?

No, but I don't want to spend the rest of my life in prison for murdering him. No way! I must think of the sort of questions the police will ask me she pondered. Yes, that's really important if I'm to get away with it. Start thinking girl!

'Where were you when he fell?'

'Did you not hear him call out? Your neighbour did.'

'Did he make any attempt to pull the shard from his neck? Did you?'

'Why didn't he try to stand up?'

'Why had you left the room? Who were you expecting for tea?' And so on.

Her answers must have satisfied the old bill and the subsequent court enquiry because his demise was registered as accidental death.

The first thing she did with the insurance money came through was to buy a complete set of Wedgewood Wild Strawberry pattern.

'Is this the same pattern as the teapot that killed Len?' her friend Gwen asked 'Doesn't it upset you using it?'

'No.' Nessa replied, smiling as she poured tea into her friend's cup. Gwen gave her a quizzical look.

Beryl Teso

THE HERB GARDEN

Many folk in the UK while delving into their family tree can trace an elderly relative who lived in a cottage in the rural countryside. My gran, despite her roots in Scotland, lived on the other side of the world.

Op de Bergen Street – the name meaning 'on the hill' was derived from the Dutch settlers who went to South Africa with Jan van Riebeeck in 1652. The house was in a suburb called Fairview – that might once have been true as it looked towards the growing city of Johannesburg. Now I would imagine the view is obliterated by many skyscrapers.

Number 17 became home to my Grandparents and their five children in the 1920s. The house had a front parlour – only used on special occasions. Further down the passage was the heart of the home.

This very large sitting/dining room contained a huge old-fashioned sofa, two matching arms chairs either side of the fireplace, a dining table for twelve places and a magnificent mahogany dresser laden with weekly cleaned silver. The bay window opposite housed many ferns highlighted by the sun filtering through the lace curtains.

The property was built early in the 1900s and the *little room* was found at the bottom of the garden. The sewage truck used to collect a container from it weekly. The family were considered posh as my grandfather had installed a bathroom with beautiful mock marble tiling. It was only in more recent times that an indoor toilet was installed.

Sunday afternoons at Nana's house were a great adventure and I discovered that this corner plot which ran at an angle had a very specific pattern of garden at the far end. It was horribly overgrown by the time I came on the scene.

A traditional herb garden had been laid out with bird bath in the centre and paths leading out like rays of the sun. There were still a few struggling plants which smelled very pungent, but no one ever ventured out to do any weeding. Nana ruled with a rod of iron and had decreed no one should touch this garden created by her deceased husband. In hindsight my gran followed the tradition of Queen Victoria. Once widowed she went into deep mourning, wearing black and occasionally purple for the remainder of her life.

At five years old I did not understand all this and would slip out to roam this wilderness. My grandfather, a builder and master plasterer had developed a method of making coloured cement pots in moulds and beautiful slabs for large mosaic pathways. It was fascinating and I would try to walk on only the pink or hop only on the green bits.

'I am very glad someone likes my handiwork.' Said the man with the wide brimmed straw hat.

He wore a waistcoat and a chain loop hung out at the side below his tweed jacket. He spoke so kindly and smiled with pride to find someone enjoying the area.

'The patterns are lovely and when I pour water on, the colours grow darker.' I replied.

On the way home I told my Mum about the man I had met.

'Now don't let your imagination run away with you.' She said, and laughing nervously, quickly changed the subject.

Many years later I was going through an old family photograph album and there was the man I had described to Mum years before.

I am proud to be the only one of the seven grandchildren who has met our grandfather, John Robert.

Gladys Lopato

WAR TOY STORY

There is a naked man lying in my front garden with his leg in the air. Weeds growing over him, and stripped of his military uniform, he doesn't look much like Action Man all. I'm watching a young Collie, she circles him, sniffing perhaps for food, or cautious of any human smell he may be hanging onto. What happened to the boy who dropped his small, vulnerable companion over my fence?

Elsewhere our War news is interrupted by earthquakes, politics, and new Wars, but here in Ukraine rubble tells the same old story. Infrastructure all around my house is broken, cables all hanging, like the dust and noxious smell the cold wind cannot filter. Apart from my little man outside, and the dog, I am the last villager remaining. When the evacuation procession passed me by, over a year ago, I stood at my gate wishing my neighbours good luck and ignoring their pleas to join them. This old woman won't travel well.

There is no food to give the dog. This hurts me like the hunger in both our bellies wakes us every day. There is some water so I will take out a dish for her to drink. I have khaki fabric so will make a new uniform for my small soldier: an eggshell can be painted for a helmet, a little stick fashioned as a gun. No boots but he can stand guard, like me, and Dog, and wait.

Wendy Ogden

THE WITCHY WOMAN

To outsiders the bayou may conjure romance. The cypress trees draped with Spanish moss, especially in the haze that hovers over the water, are icons of these parts. To outsiders, but not always to those who call them home. The bayous and swamps are mysterious places. When the sun's gold is elbowed away by the moonlight and the lazy breeze flutters through the moss, they appear another world, another time.

Parents tell their children not to venture too far into the swamp. Alligators may ambush and their victims be dragged down into the depths - never to be seen again. They warn other creatures lurk there too; creatures not of this world. As children we believe our parents - as we get older and braver we are more likely to heed our peers. The threat of danger, of the unknown, begins to evaporate even in the mystical atmosphere of the bayou.

At twelve my fear began to evaporate. Denny and Lucas, at two years older than me, had already grown fearless; fearless enough to want to find out about the strange woman who lived in the cabin that fronted the creek. We had all wondered about her. She arrived like a hurricane in a beat-up old flatbed truck. The ramshackle cabin that had lain empty for a long time became her home. What, if any, connection it had with her we never found out.

The local busybody approached to ask while she was loading the truck in town one day but a dismissive wave of the hand and a throaty chuckle was her only reply. We wanted to check her out for ourselves. The way to the cabin took as along a muddy track just off the creek road. To follow was too difficult though as the truck could cope with the mud but our sneakers couldn't. Even if we had made it to the cabin all we would be able to see was the back so Denny came up with a plan. He would borrow his dad's field glasses and we would hide on the other side of the creek opposite the shack. We would be safe, she wouldn't know we were watching, we could find out what goes on there. Folk suspected there were nefarious goings on. I didn't know what the word nefarious meant but judging by the hushed tones in which it was spoken I suspected it was something dodgy.

We slipped off after supper. I told my mom I was going to Lucas's house, got my flashlight and went to meet my friends. We needed to be in place before sunset because 'what went on' started around sunset - according to the whispers. Going through the trees in the almost dark was spooky - rustling among the shadows. There was just enough light to make our way and hopefully catch the Witchy Woman. What her name was we never found out and I had never seen her before that night. The nickname we lifted from the Eagles' song and it suited her well according to her description by those who had seen her; raven black hair and ruby red lips. In the song the Witchy

Woman was driven to madness with the silver spoon. What that meant then I didn't know. I do now of course. Her cabin was in view. We got settled. The mist on the water made it appear to be floating, hovering. Lanterns hung along the porch, coloured lanterns that gave the porch an eerie glow - their reflections dancing on the mirror water of the creek.

We couldn't see her, not yet, but could hear movement and barely whispering through the almost still air, wind chimes. Denny studied them through the field glasses then passed them to me so I could do the same. They were unlike any I had seen before and definitely did not come from the local hardware store. No way. There were shells and sticks and beads and a silvery spoon like in the song and bones; bones larger than the other items that hung there. Where had the bones come from? Had she killed something? Or someone? I shuddered. We all shuddered.

Then from inside came voices, laughter; crazy laughter. Not just hers alone but a man's voice, maybe two men's voices. They came out. Yes, two men. They flopped down onto an old worn settee - frayed and dirty like a tired, lumbering animal but they didn't care; they looked at home. We could just about make out what they were saying. I remember.

'Where is it? Bring that sweet stuff out here honey – the best'.

'Always the best here; y'know everything you get here is the best.'

She laughed and this laugh was unlike anything I had heard from a woman. I still can't explain it. She sashayed out carrying a glass flagon and swilled the contents round and round before pouring it into mugs and handing it to the men. She was very beautiful and wore a red dress that my mom would regard as indecent. Our eyes popped. Lucas thought he recognised one of the men but couldn't be sure. Perhaps just as well. Moonshine, the flagon contained moonshine. Lots of illegal stills hidden away deep among the cypresses and the good stuff didn't come cheap. I recall listening to mom and dad talking about Witchy and how she got hold of it and with no means of support - how she paid. She must have 'reciprocal arrangements' they decided. As with nefarious I had no idea what that meant but clearly do now.

When the men finished downing two mugs full the biggest one stubbed out his cigarette among the parched flowers in the lopsided window box and they drifted, staggered, inside. She went in last; she paused, didn't actually look round but wagged her finger behind her. It was as if she knew she was being watched and, maybe, warning us off. Lucas and Denny were fidgeting - they didn't notice, but I did. We waited awhile as some odd noises emanated out - noises we were not familiar with - but decided we better scoot home before the darkness closed in completely. We didn't speak about that night. It was our secret.

Soon after she was no longer around. She disappeared as suddenly as she had arrived. No one saw her or her truck in town. There were no gossip snippets about her exploits - imagined or real. She seemed to have vanished. No one was really surprised. No one really cared - well some did but they weren't telling. Me, Denny and Lucas decided to visit the cabin - this time along the now dried up track. We dared despite being scared what we would find. It was me who pushed the door. It creaked open. It wasn't locked. We went inside. Empty. Nothing. We went onto the porch. Stuffing poked out of the old settee and mice had made their home inside. The window box held a multitude of cigarette butts among the long dead plants. The wind chimes, however, no longer hung on the nail where we saw them.

We left kind of disappointed; nothing dramatic to see. What I expected I don't know. Denny expected a body – a rotting corpse he said. Although if that had been the case I think he would have fainted. Maybe given what he went on to do for a job perhaps not though.

All that happened over twenty years ago. I left for a corporate job in St Louis, got married, got divorced and came back to visit my parents from time to time. Just before my last visit a monumental storm caused havoc over the bayou. Not a hurricane fortunately because they are always a threat in this part of the country. That was why I came - to make sure mom and dad were ok. The thunder, lightning, heavy rain and wind had passed now. The oppressive heat had returned to suffocate everything living and the air moved not an inch.

Whilst on this visit I met up with Denny. He moved away to become a police officer in New Orleans, also married but stayed married. On his return he became elevated to Chief of Police. Lucas had moved up north so there was just the two of us to reminisce about our childhood and the time we spied on the mysterious Witchy Woman. Was the cabin still standing? I asked him. Apparently so and only visited by boys about the same age as we were or teenagers up to nefarious purposes of their own. Witchy had never returned. We would go visit, for old time's sake.

As Denny and I stood on the side of the creek where we had spied from all those years ago, we could hear wind chimes. Hear them clearly; the sound chimes make when the breeze is strong. The sound they shouldn't be making at all in the stillness - even if they were there. But they weren't there and hadn't been since she disappeared. Why, if they no longer hung, could we hear them? It was as if they were calling us somehow – summoning us. We felt compelled to get closer but the jangling appeared to move. It wafted further away from the cabin and along the creek. Denny and I looked at each other in puzzlement but followed to where the road nudged the creek further along from the cabin. The creek had been disturbed by the storm. Trees and even rocks had been lifted and moved; trees and rocks that had lain still for some twenty odd years.

We drove round to the other side, parked up and made our way down to the water's edge ignoring the splashes of disturbed alligators. Showing above the chocolate swamp water like one unseeing eye, poked a headlight; the corner of a truck. It must have been dislodged from its watery tomb by the storm. Denny radioed for a team. The truck - an old flatbed - was lifted. The wind chimes faded away as we made our discovery. Neither of us imagined this. It was real.

On the floor of the cab, Denny later told me, next to the remains of Witchy Woman lay a scattering of shells and beads and a rusty spoon and ... bones. The sticks and string had long since rotted away but the bones had rested alongside hers all these years. Now we finally knew what happened to Witchy Woman. What we don't know and never will, is how non-existent wind chimes playing on non-existent wind led us to her grave.

Jackie Harvey

MEMORIES OF MANDY

Mandy and I lived together for a little over four years. I'm still not sure that was her name, she never told me. I just called her Mandy. It was a very happy liaison of minds. We met while both shopping at a department store. I was there for a specific reason and Mandy was, I believe, there just for window shopping. I didn't particularly notice her amongst the other window shoppers. I was an easy pickup and I could have been anyone male, female or other, she didn't really care who I was. She was also an easy pickup; I wasn't fussed one way or another. I was lonely and she was gorgeous looking. After some hard negotiation and some monetary exchange, we both went home together. I said my place or yours, she wasn't bothered so we went to mine.

She was a bit of a hippy and had a kind of shawl, or sarong wrapped around her. I said you need some clothes. Then I remembered the wardrobe upstairs which was full of clothes that Joy had left when she moved out. Mandy and I had great fun rummaging through them and trying them on. All the costumes fitted her perfectly. The boots made her look like Pussy Galore in Goldfinger, and I quickly covered her naked body with an ankle length coat. Luckily, we found some nice underwear, although a little too sexy for my liking. After quite a tiring day

Mandy found a nice pair of warm fleecy all in one pyjamas and I put on my boring hospital stripy ones.

We woke up early and decided to go swimming. Mandy found a bathing suit and swimmers cap in the wardrobe and we headed off to a secluded beach. Mandy wasn't much of a swimmer but did enjoy just floating around on her back. Even though we didn't talk much on that beautiful day, in that beautiful place, our relationship grew strong. We just knew we were meant for each other. I kept hinting to Mandy to get the barbeque going for lunch, she just lay there sunbathing. I ended up lighting the barby, cooking the food, clearing up and then driving us home. When we got home Mandy took off her bathing suit and swimming cap and decided to put all the jewellery on that she found in the wardrobe. It did look fabulous on her amazing body, but I insisted she draped the Union Jack flag, we had in the hall, around her for modesty and warmth. We continued our non-verbal communication for the next few years in total harmony. I did love her. I continued doing all the housework, all the cooking, all the washing, all the shopping and gardening. In fact, I did everything, and Mandy just watched in total silence, but this did not affect our perfect relationship.

Eventually though, love had run its course and so we parted ways when I put an advert on Facebook Marketplace offering 'Mannequin for Sale'.

Denis MacReever

PSYCHIC

Being psychic was a bit of a mixed blessing, Betty thought, and not for the first time. She never really knew whether it was a blessing or a curse. Certainly, she had made a comfortable living at it, but she had long realised that it was probably better for people not to know what was ahead of them. As far as she knew the whole point of life was working it out for yourself, making mistakes and learning. Fortune telling, although in her case, hugely accurate, was a bit of a cheat.

Most people want reassurance about the future, anyway, and plainly that was not always possible. Into every life a little rain must fall… She never needed the tarot cards, they were just something to focus on while her mind went off somewhere, seeing things clearly. Some things you really couldn't be honest about. Who wants to know they would be widowed before they were thirty?

No. Now she only did psychometry. So much easier, after all the past was the past, nothing would change that. Plus, she enjoyed it. Far better than television, Netflix even. This was a blessing indeed. To go back in time, to see, smell and watch history in the making, to actually be a witness to times gone by and experience it. Wonderful, she could never get enough. It was definitely a drop in money, but she was comfortable. She had her cottage, and her pets, and her herbs and her books, she was very content. Far better than that illusive happy thing that usually came before disappointment.

She held up the brooch that her last client had given her. Probably Victorian, oh dear, she was a bit bored with Victorian, all those horses with black plumes pulling carriages, and the workhouse was not a place she enjoyed visiting. She needed to be realistic, however, she could hardly say no to her clients, whatever they brought her. She would have preferred something a bit older though.

Betty settled in her chair by the fire and as soon as she tuned in to the brooch, she surprisedly felt quite happy being immediately transported to the countryside, really quite tranquil and peaceful this time. She looked around her. It must be sunrise, almost light, no-one about although she was obviously on a farm. She could see the farmhouse ahead of her, with chickens outside and a horse in the barn. She was in a hurry, going to the house almost running. She couldn't run properly as her knees hurt and she got out of breath easily.

Looking down on herself, she saw long skirts tangling around her legs, her basket was full of something, but covered in a cloth, she saw veined hands, withered arms. She was obviously quite old, very old in fact, feeling all kinds of aches and pains now. There, as Betty looked down on herself, was the brooch, somehow cobbling her blouse together over long hung breasts. Well at least she now knew who it belonged to.

She reached the farmhouse and opened the door. An old dog snuffled towards her, wagging its tail. She was known here then. 'Upstairs!' Someone shouted, so up the old rickety stairs she slowly climbed. Oh, of course, she realised, she was the midwife! Her granddaughter writhed on the old bed, panting swearing and sweating. Well, the first is often the worst, she thought, as she retrieved the herbal tinctures from her basket. But what a joy! To deliver your first great grandchild, no wonder she felt so happy. No wonder she felt old!

Then, suddenly, she was back in her chair by the fire. Well, that was a nice one, she thought, but it would have been good to see if it was a boy or girl. She couldn't go back though. She never could. Nice to tell the client though. Where did she find that brooch? It might well have been a family piece. She could find out later. Now the fire was cold, it was time for bed. She must have been away longer than she thought.

Jane Kenton-Wright

FREEDOM

I was walking through the town yesterday thinking about nothing except what to buy for dinner when I noticed the figure of a man crossing the road just ahead of me. For some reason the shape of him struck a chord – albeit a discordant one.

I did a double take – no it just couldn't be, I'm mistaken. The word was that after at least twenty-five years with neither sight nor sound of him and a clairvoyant declaring "he had passed" he must have. I'm not a particular believer in the art but in this instance, I was willing to take the word of a clairvoyant. More a case of wishful thinking and I make no apologies for verbalising that feeling.

It was with some trepidation that I took, one may say, a dangerous step and crossed the road to follow him to see if my eyes had deceived me – please God they had.

My mind was abounding with conflict, questioning the sense in following, but I pressed on. I definitely didn't want him to see me, but I definitely wasn't about to waste this excellent opportunity - handed to me on a plate - to lay all the unanswered questions to rest as to whether he was dead or alive. You could be forgiven for asking why follow him, why put myself at risk of being seen, but this man, if it was him, had hurt and terrorised me and mine for years. Sometimes, however many years later, you have to know for sure, as in this case. I needed peace of mind and to lay some serious ghosts to rest.

Whilst following him, albeit with a degree of hesitancy, as we left the town centre with less busy streets, I began to feel a lot less confident about the rightness of following him. By now I was that convinced it was him – six-foot tall, slim, broad shouldered, upper body redolent of a piece of Toblerone, long legs, curly hair with barely any grey but the giveaway for me was the spring-like walk. Yep, it was definitely him.

I was going to miss my doctor's appointment, but I didn't care. My entire being was focused on him. Suddenly he stopped, turned and there he was, facing me – no escape. Literally or metaphorically. Thirty-six years ago this man had broken into my house, nearly killed me, left me with many injuries, eventual surgery and nothing but fear. Memories I would never erase.

Evil comes in many guises but there is none so bad as the one that once upon a time had promised to love you, cherish you and take care of you.

When I looked at him, I felt that old terrible gut-wrenching fear almost take me over again – but then I looked more closely. He'd always been a vain, arrogant man with regard to his looks and physique but the only thing that was still the same was his size. He had no teeth, his skin was grey scaly and wrinkled, the curly hair was a wig which was slightly askew at the front. In that moment, just as he was about to speak, all the years of fear and loathing and wishing this man harm ended – just like that – in the blink of an eye.

    I laughed and laughed – I just couldn't stop myself – to say he was stunned was a minor understatement especially as I just turned and walked away with a massive smile on my face and the frivolous uncharitable thought that popped into my head was – it's true – *karma really is a bitch.*

Susan Cooper

DANUBE DELTA DRAMA - A TRUE LIFE STORY

Watching a frog hopping along the boat's veranda in front of me, I was enjoying the feel of the sun on my body, trying to push the memory of the previous day from my mind. Then, a pair of boots and combat trousered legs appeared in front of me. My eyes travelled upwards.
Into the barrel of a gun.

An unsmiling soldier. I jumped up. He motioned me around the corner. Not a word spoken, but when someone has a gun and you do not, it is amazing how much sign language you understand. I joined the rest of the party and two more soldiers, on deck. Two boats were moored behind ours.

A tannoy crackled and our interpreter, in three languages - English, French and German, ordered everyone who, including my husband, had gone ashore, to return.

I had been ill and under the doctor's suggestion a proper holiday would improve my recovery. With our two children cared for by friends, this cheapie holiday seemed the answer. Knowing nothing of this country's politics, little did we realise as our boat glided down the Danube, that the events of the last, and following few days, would haunt us for years to come. This was Romania, 1975 and Nicolae Ceausescu was in power.

Excitedly, our party had spilled off the coach that brought us from our hotel in Mamaia. Most had cameras and notebooks. This was to be a three-day trip to the Danube Delta, an amazing wetland, home to over 300 species of birds and 1,150 kinds of plants. Conversations were solely of flora and fauna, political problems were the last things on our minds.

Our attractive courier introduced himself as Jon. Smartly dressed, his bright eyes, ready smile, and charming manner were endearing. Happily, we settled into our seats and Jon pointed out things of interest as we drifted lazily along. Eating the picnics provided, there were some comments about the unimaginative contents of our packages, but, on the whole, we were a contented lot.

Suddenly, the boat stopped, gliding towards the bank. Enquiring faces turned to Jon. What was happening? Why this unscheduled halt? His smile had gone. He looked serious and his eyes held a flash of rage. My mouth turned dry. What was wrong?

'So far on your holiday you have seen the Cultural things our government want you to see. But now I will show you what they are hiding. Follow me and see how my people really live.'

We looked at each other in consternation as he repeated the message in German and French. As he climbed out, we were afraid to follow, but even more afraid to stay without him. Reluctantly, we helped each other clamber onto the bank. As we walked through the reeds, dark, smelly slime oozed through the toes of my sandals, slid under my soles, and out through the backs. I wrinkled my nose with horror and disgust as I realised this was not mud, but sewage.

Others shared my disgust, though no one spoke. We emerged and stood in a confused huddle looking at a collection of wooden shacks each with a plot of vegetables beside it. Why did Jon want to show us allotments?

'This is my home village,' said Jon quietly. 'Go in pairs to the houses, the people will show you their homes.'

Homes?! Silently we obeyed. The shack we chose did not have a door. Instead, a sheet of black rubber, similar to that used to line garden ponds here in England, hung from the lintel. A gnarled hand emerged and pulled it aside. Nervously, we stepped into the gloomy interior. It took a few moments to adjust, the only light coming from one small glassless window and the smoke-hole above. The floor was of hard earth. In a corner, a bed. To one side, a stove. A wide shelf, heaped with blankets, sat above it. Another shelf containing, pans, vegetables and bread, ran around the remainder of the room. A mouse nibbled at the loaf. The packed lunch, about which some of us had complained, turned in my stomach.

The owner of the gnarled hand, a skinny, elderly woman with lined face and drab, stained clothes, studied me with dead eyes. I glanced at my sewage-stained sandals and my chain store 'cheapie' clothes. Gucci compared with hers. I felt embarrassed. The equally elderly and shabby man beside her, attempted a welcoming smile; his few remaining blackened teeth turned it into a grimace.

The blanket heap on the stove-shelf moved, I heard giggles. A child's face peeped out, followed by another. This was where children slept for warmth. Their thin faces were dirt-streaked but lively. Knowing no other life than this they retained a modicum of childhood innocence. But for how much longer? I thought of my own children, about the same age as these. A furnished bedroom each; a choice of clothing in the wardrobe. And we considered ourselves far from wealthy. I realised with a jolt the elderly looking couple were their parents and therefore probably no older than myself and my husband even though they looked much older. My hand reached out to touch a child but withdrew rapidly as I saw the flea that leapt from his hair, settled momentarily on his cheek and jumped into the blanket.

We left and rejoined the equally shocked members of my party. There was much I wanted to ask Jon. How had he escaped from all this? But how can you ask someone such questions when you cannot meet his eye?

Silently we retraced our steps, wading uncomplainingly through the sewage to the boat. The sun still shone, but it had lost its warmth and brightness; the plants and birds had lost their magical quality. We were pleased to arrive at the hotel, meet our interpreter and be greeted by a smiling, jovial Manager.

Attempting to eradicate the memories of the day, we all drank more than we should and slept soundly – only to awake next morning with thumping heads and flea-bitten bodies. But after what we had seen, our complaints via the interpreter to the ever-smiling Manager, were not particularly vociferous. And a further shock that made us forget all parasitic irritations, awaited us.

Once everyone was accounted for, we were commanded to collect our belongings. We would be returning to our main hotels in half an hour. This brought protests from the foolhardy.

'We have another day. Where is our Courier?'

'Your Courier has been arrested,' barked the interpreter, gesturing to one of the boats that was moving away. 'You will be returned to the coaches and your hotels immediately. You will speak to no-one about this.'

'How will we know which coach is ours?' asked one man. 'We cannot read Romanian.'

'This man will escort you.'

'He is the hotel Manager and speaks no English.'
I looked at the still-smiling face. A smile that no longer reached the cold, blue eyes. The Manager was also a member of the dreaded Securitate.

The Departamentual Securitatii Statului, usually known as the Securitate, was then Romania's Secret Political Police. They had informants everywhere to report on the anti-regime activities and opinions of ordinary citizens and workers. Jon was now in their hands for showing us his village. Several members of our party, including myself, wept silently. Another courier was placed on our boat and the Manager joined the soldiers on the other.

'Please help my friend,' whispered our new Courier, 'tell the Authorities he is a good representative for Romania.'

'Have you asked the French or Germans?' we whispered back.

'No, only you. It's known the English are always on the side of the underdog.'

Our group held a quiet debate and reached a conclusion.

'We dare not help. Your Authorities hold our passports.' He nodded with sad understanding.
I was ashamed.

Disembarking, we were delighted to see Jon waiting. But joy was short-lived. This was a very different Jon. His drawn face was pale, the smile no more than a muscle twitch. His eyes seemed unfocused and although there were no marks to be seen, the way he held his body it was obvious he had taken a beating.

'Do not talk about anything you have seen or heard,' he commanded in a croaking voice as he saw us on to our coaches, then in a whisper, 'but in England tell everyone what happens here.'

He was marched away.

We were relieved to be on the coaches but noticed we had extra passengers. One at the back, one to the front. We heeded Jon's words and did not discuss our experiences. As people shared sweets and cigarettes these two refused everything with a curt shake of the head. When we arrived in Mamaia they melted into the crowd.

The hotel staff must have been told something, none seemed surprised we were back early, yet none seemed to want to look directly at us. As the holiday continued, we frequently bumped into people who had been on the trip. In open spaces where we could not be overheard, we asked the same question. Who were the extra passengers? Everyone had the same feeling, had we discussed those events in English, French or German they would have understood - and there would have been repercussions.

I knew that returning home, I would be grateful for the life we have in England. And I have responded to Jon's request and talked about those dramatic days in the Danube Delta to students in College and University.

But what actually happened to Jon, I dread to think.

Veronica Allerston

BEHIND CLOSED DOORS

My beloved grandparents lived in Cornwall and, as a child, I always used to stay with them during my summer holiday. But childhood is just a brief interlude in our lives, and before you know it the daily grind of caring for the family: going to work, and paying the mortgage take over, so sadly I rarely got to see them once I had grown up..
****

Mum phoned me today to tell me the sad news that my lovely grandma had 'joined her husband in heaven.' Mmm! Not sure about that, but if it makes her happy, who am I to challenge her.

We travelled down to Cornwall the following day to arrange her funeral. Reminiscing about them on the journey we remembered the strange phone call mum had from granny, many years ago, to tell us that grandpa had died. She only told her about it ten days after his death and said he had already been cremated. My Mother was very upset at the time as she rightly felt she should have been there for her father's funeral, and it caused bad feeling between them for a couple of years.

We buried grandma in the cemetery on the hill; along with generations of Pascoes, Chegwins and Trevelyans. Fishermen, tin miners, and their wives, had been laid to rest there, going back to the sixteenth century. The sort of funeral grandpa should have had instead of being cremated.

Bless her; granny left her cottage to me in her will. It needed a massive clean-up, so I took a week off work in order to do this and think about what I wanted to do with it in the future. There is a little attic room in the roof where I used to sleep when I stayed with them. I loved it for its fantastic views of the sea and the beautiful surrounding countryside, but for some reason the door was locked. Odd I thought, but it was her home and was up to her what she did in it. I thought no more about it. I'd found a bunch of keys but there didn't appear to be one that fitted that particular lock, but later cleaning up the dresser, I found a key under the drawer lining which looked as if it might fit. I wondered why it wasn't on the main bunch. Why had granny hidden it?

Yes, it fitted. I carefully unlocked the door to the darkened room. It had a peculiarly sweet, musty, unpleasant smell, caused by the lack of fresh air over the years I assumed. I couldn't find the light switch, so went across to the window and drew the back the curtains which fell to bits the minute I touched them. I looked around my old bedroom lovingly at first. The bed was made neatly as if a guest was expected – then, I screamed and couldn't get out of the room fast enough. I half ran half fell down the stairs taking them three at a time and tumbled down the last half dozen crashing onto the floor.

I picked myself up, grabbed the phone and called the police. I was shaking so much I could barely speak.

'Sorry ma'am I can't understand you.'
The policeman said.

'I have just found my grandfather's fully clothed skeleton - still with his trilby hat on- sitting in a chair in the attic room of my grandma's cottage.' I gabbled. 'He's been dead for at least twelve years. Please come quickly.'

Beryl Teso

THE LOTTERY

It was a permutation that had always captured me. A series of numbers that each week I would religiously check hoping to win the big one and this had gone on for years. I would be a rich woman, if I'd just kept the stake, but where was the fun in that? You can bet if I didn't do them, they'd soon come up then.

It was all very costly. I would always use my mum and dad's birthdays. And, my son's and three sisters. Plus, a few other numbers that had a significant meaning for me, which equated to several lines. Still, just think, if I did get the big one, can you imagine the celebration.

I would decorate my pad from top to bottom with all the best gear, and I'm sure I could afford designer too. It needed a good makeover anyway. I just didn't have the money right now. Still, with that massive windfall, I could probably buy a new place and in a much better area.

But I liked it here, it had good vibes. Over the years I would drift from one place to another, and never really settled down anywhere. It would be great to lay some roots.

My boyfriend, Yan, had never wanted to stay in one area for too long. Of course, it took me a while to realise why. But the smell of cannabis growing in one of the bedrooms should have really told me.

The deceit of the man was unspeakable. Mind you, I quite liked the smell in the end, you kind of get used to it. Although Yan, would often come out in a fever during the night. I didn't understand why at the time, but he was obviously having withdrawals. It affects people differently apparently.

He had another woman you know. And when the cops turned up, after someone reported this pungent smell, oozing from our flat, it was off to hers that he ran. Leaving me and my son to face the music.

My son was really upset when Yan left. But I managed to bribe him with talk of a big win, one day soon. I told him - life will be much better then. If only. He's forgotten all about him now, thankfully. He wasn't his dad anyway.

I must say, it was certainly satisfying when they caught him in the end. Gave him five years too. When I heard, I couldn't stop laughing. God knows what his bit on the side thinks now. I wonder if it's been a time of great tribulation or relief.

Still, we were all taken in. Yan had the gift of the gab, but no more. Prison hopefully will teach him a lesson or two. Although thanks to him I've certainly learnt a lot and my harvest has been more than plentiful. It's funny how popular you can suddenly become when one has the means to bring on the highs. Perhaps I don't need those numbers after all.

Lena Bowling

THE HOLIDAY

As the fluffy white clouds, dark at the edges, parted, rays of sunshine made her eyes sting. The woman on the rock shifted to make herself more comfortable. The sea beyond was turbulent. Pieces of blue sky started appearing.

The woman would have described her mood as blue but how strange that the blue of the sky looked so beautiful. However, she had never felt more alone. Perhaps there was hope. Perhaps it would be all right. She had felt she had no choice.

As her tears made ripples in the water and bounced on some dead wood floating past, any drifting thoughts were interrupted by her black Labrador crunching through the pebbles on the beach then sniffing round the bottom of the rock.

****

Clare had noticed the woman in the garden that led down to the edge of the water on the loch. She had been sitting in her favourite place which was in the window of the large bedroom in the country house hotel. Dusk fell late in the Scottish Highlands and the mountains beyond and behind the small copse had turned black. Clare noticed the dark Labrador as it padded to pick up the ball that the woman had thrown. She seemed to be alone as Clare had first noticed her leaving the breakfast room as she and her husband, Rob, entered. There was a cheery 'Good morning' between them before she was gone. Clare had seen her again exercising the dog just before they went out.

Over the next few days, the routine was the same. Clare and Rob, an unremarkable younger retired couple, went out walking on vast deserted sand beaches overlooked by mountains. Here, Clare felt alive and free. She felt better connected with Rob and they shared happy moments surrounded by beauty.

There were places where islands in the middle could be waded to through shallow waters. Clare often found herself on one, the water lapping gently. She would gaze at the stunning view and try and focus her thoughts on the forthcoming celebration of her daughter's engagement.

However, she struggled to fully accept this with the knowledge of the fiancé's deceit. Clare had laboured over every permutation. What was her daughter thinking of to commit to a man who was a gambler and addict? The cost in all ways had been huge but as far as her daughter was concerned, that was all in the past and he had changed. Did people change? Rob certainly hadn't. In truth, his annoying stubborn ways had got worse over the years.

Clare found her mind wandering back to the woman with the dog, probably in her mid to late seventies – no husband, partner or companion – just her and the dog. Did she normally holiday alone? Was she lonely? Where did she live? Why was she so fascinated? Did this reflect Clare's own empty life?

They had exchanged pleasantries most days, often in the hall with the antique pieces on the sideboards. Clare loved the small hotel with its wonderful old rooms, creaky floorboards and high ceilings.

She and Rob enjoyed a drink each evening in the drawing room with the comfy sofas. They often chatted to a young couple who were climbing the Munros. He loved the challenge but she found it an endurance. How different people were, Clare thought, and what they would put themselves through to please or indulge the other. Much like herself and Rob.

The owner of the hotel, Giles, was passionate about creating a homely environment, beautiful comfortable rooms and he loved cooking dinner for his guests. The woman didn't join the others. Perhaps she ate in her room to keep the dog company.

On their last evening, as Clare and Rob came down the wide oak staircase, they were met by a flustered Giles. He apologised that dinner would be a bit late as he had needed to call a doctor for one of his guests who had a high fever.

As Clare was packing up the last things the next morning for their departure home, she looked for the woman out of the window. There were colourful little boats bobbing in the water moored up near the shore.

The breeze was getting up and the mountains were clear against the sky.

The journey home was long but the scenery was outstanding, though a bit foreboding as the rain had started to lash down. Plenty of time, as the windscreen wipers fought to clear the rain, to reflect on life's trials and tribulations.

Home was a neat suburban semi where a lot of days were the same. Clare and Rob got through the days. The newspaper was delivered each morning and before Clare made herself busy in the house or set of for her various activities or commitments, she would sit at the kitchen table and flick through, skimming anything that particularly caught her attention.

A couple of weeks after their return and the holiday seeming a distant memory as monotonous routine had resumed, some headlines caught her eye:

'Woman holidays leaving husband with dementia to die alone in the attic'.

Caroline Scotter

TRAPPED

There was no other way out. None. He had wracked his brains for another solution but nothing else could be done. He would have to ask for help - something he finds completely alien. 'I am my own man – I do not need anyone to guide or guard me. Anyone who does is weak.' That is what he thinks, what he believes – been brought up to believe by a father who drove him into the countryside at eight years old, told him to find his way back, and left him. Sure, he made it and his father was pleased - at least he seemed pleased - and from that day on he would place his trust in no one.

His father and mother were around until he was seventeen until, without warning, they told him they were going to travel - to 'find themselves.' From that moment he was on his own.

He never saw them again. Until now. Ten years later he heard from his mother out of the blue. How she found him he couldn't imagine. He had moved around - all over the country and beyond. Done this and that, here and there. Not put down any roots as this would involve other people - even trusting other people. He couldn't do that; been conditioned not to.

His mother called him and said they had to meet. Somehow, she had obtained his number. What about father, where was he? No answer - just meet. So, they did. A cafe by a park, on a corner. She looked the same yet different, having aged more than she should have. Her hair was obviously dyed, her face drawn, her manner nervous. She stood when he approached appearing unsteady, seemingly uncomfortable seeing her only son after so long.

He looked well. Was he well? She asked. A shrug was his reply, he didn't even know himself if he truly was. What did she want, why now? Where was father? She was jumpy - looking around expecting someone or something. She said she needed his help. And quickly.

Why? What could he do? And after all this time why should he? He could take something for them and look after it until they could collect it. Collect what? What is in the package? She wouldn't say but not for long just until...Until what? When? Just until... she hesitantly answered.

Against his better judgement and, despite being estranged for so long, she was still his mother so he agreed. That is why he is in this position. Not knowing what to do, who to turn to. They have left him again. In a corner – caught between a rock and a hard place, the devil and the deep blue sea. Old clichés but unfortunately true. Why should he have any loyalty to them? What had they got him mixed up in? Something not good – he could sense it.

Should he go to the police? To tell them what though? His parents could be in deep trouble. Whatever the package was - and she told him not to look - it had to be dodgy. No way out except the police. Tell them everything, give them the package. Out of his hands. If his parents go down or if, and maybe worse, whoever they are involved with catches up with them, that's not his problem.

Once his father left him to make his own way and he did. He owes them nothing, absolutely nothing, so now he would leave them to find their own way through whatever they had gotten themselves into. Probably a trap entirely of their own making. Retribution, perhaps, at long last.

Jackie Harvey

RECYCLING

'I'm a firm believer in recycling.' Mrs Pogmore, her chins trembling in smug agreement, continued, 'I'll dispose of everything before I leave.'

I heard her emphasise the last two words as if to remind her visitors and me - of her impending adventure and that we would remain in our unexciting lives.

'Hurry, Martha,' she called, 'our cups need refilling.'

The screen was placed in front of the kitchen door so that her guests should not see me working. I was supposed to emerge silently from behind it with trays of tea and cakes and equally silently withdraw. It also provided me with the means of spying and eavesdropping while I waited for the kettle to boil. Everyone needs a hobby, and this is mine.

'Who knows, I may find myself another rich husband on the Cruise and never return to England!' Mrs Pogmore continued, giggling girlishly.

'Probably will,' I heard Ada Green mutter with an emotion to match her name, 'how's she managed to find two already and I haven't found one?'

'How does she always find the ones with money and a short lifespan?' whispered Irene Wills.

To console herself, Ada stretched out a scrawny hand towards the last cream cake. Too late; Irene was faster, her podgy hand knocking Ada Green's dirty finger into the current bun at its side. Ada licked her finger and settled for the flapjack.

The kettle whistled and I returned to the kitchen, warmed the teapot and spooned in the tea. With practiced skill, I spat into the pot before pouring in the water. A small gesture but so satisfactory. I carried the tray in and poured the tea wishing my spit carried some contagious disease that would infect them all.

I glanced from the window at the land that had been a thriving smallholding and Ernest Pogmore's pride and joy. Now it was barren, awaiting the developers who had paid his widow a hefty price.

'Just the pig to be collected now,' continued Mrs Pogmore, 'I've given that to Mr Marsh.'

'You haven't given it to him he's paid you for it.' I thought crossly as I returned to the kitchen.

I knew this as my second job was with him in exchange for the two-up two-down cottage I shared with my mother. At the end of my hours with Mrs Pogmore, I would cycle down the hill to Mr Marsh's abattoir and cut joints for sale in his shop the following day. Every evening I chopped and sliced.

'.Strong as any man in spite of your tiny frame,' he often told me.

I returned to my hiding place and put my eye to the crack in the screen. Mrs Pogmore was still babbling.

'In fact, I'm so organised with my plans, I might leave early and stay in a nice hotel being pampered before we sail.'

She continued beaming at her guests.

Ada managed to turn her disgusted snort into a polite cough.

'Thanks for the tea', said Irene presently, 'I must go I've work to do. Want a lift, Ada?'

After I had cleared the debris and washed up, Mrs Pogmore handed me a paper bag.

'You may take this home, I don't believe in waste', she said with a generous air.

Opening it, I gazed at the curling slices of bread and the currant bun, the imprint of Ada's finger clearly visible. Not allowing my face to display my disgust I accepted it silently. Mounting my bike, I threw the bag and its contents into the sty as I passed. The pig was not particular and munched it happily, bag and all.

I have a sunny nature and my black mood had lifted by the time I had reached the abattoir. I worked diligently all evening. Cutting, chopping and slicing.

As time passed, my workload did not lessen. Although most of the furniture was sold, Mrs Pogmore would often make me re-polish the remaining pieces in order to get her full money's worth from me. Occasionally she would give me some worthless knick-knack with the air of Royalty bestowing largesse to the peasants.

When you are poor you learn to make the best of things and some pieces could be used. The jug made a pretty vase if its chipped lip faced the wall. The blunt embroidery scissors responded well to the whetstone. And there was the soap to which Mrs Pogmore was allergic. Once the odd hair had been removed and I had peeled off the used layer with the potato peeler, and wrapped it in tissue, topped with a bow from a chocolate box, it was accepted with delight by my invalid mother. I watched her with a look of pleasure and sadness. Why did Mrs P. have so much and my beloved mother so little? My resentment grew. But it was the bloomers that finally did it. As I dusted the landing rail post, Mrs Pogmore bustled from the bedroom waving something pink, like a flag.

'For your mother,' she said flapping a pair of huge bloomers that had seen better days, in my face.

The mental picture of my frail mother swathed in something so enormous could have been hilarious had it not been so insulting. Even had they not been several sizes too big, could Mrs Pogmore really think my mother had so little pride she would wear someone else's cast-off bloomers?

But there was a lot of lace around the legs. Unpicked and laundered it would brighten up the edges of a couple of mother's plain nightdresses. So, with a tight smile, I accepted them.

'Just a moment,' said Mrs Pogmore, snatching the obscene garment back, 'I'll take the lace off, it's too good to waste.'

I shouldn't have done it but rage boiled up and overflowed like a volcano's eruption. I lashed out at her feeling my man-strong hands make contact with the soft, spongy flesh of her chest and I pushed with all my strength. The human mountain that was my employer, wobbled, steadied, wobbled towards me. I panicked, and pushed her away again.

With a look of astonishment on her face, Mrs Pogmore toppled slowly backwards down the stairs. There was a series of loud shrieks as she bounced making contact with every stair, her arms clutching unsuccessfully at each banister rung. Her skirt ballooned; I caught sight of her fat legs sticking out from her expensive knickers. Then thud, splat. She landed on the hall floor.

Looking dishevelled and harassed I arrived late for my evening shift and apologised. Mr Marsh waved my apology to one side.

'It's the first time you've been late, and no doubt that awful Pogmore female has kept you working.' He beamed at me. 'Soon we'll have you all to ourselves.'

I smiled back. Once my notice had been worked out at Mrs Pogmore's, in addition for the cottage in exchange for the evening work, I was to help Mrs Marsh in their house for a proper wage. The added bonus being I would be on hand for Mother. Grateful for his tolerance, I tucked my untidy hair into its net and set to work chopping and slicing.

In the three weeks before my contract expired, it was amazing how many of Mrs Pogmore's gifts I managed to take home either in my bicycle panniers or strapped to the crossbar. There was a dinner service — the first time my mother had owned six matching plates — and some cutlery and a lace tablecloth. Also cushions, a mirror and pictures. On Saturdays when I didn't go to the abattoir, I took the longer route round the edge of the valley pushing a handcart. The first time it contained a small bookcase, the second a bathroom cabinet and a bedside chair. It was hard work and took time, but for the look of sheer delight on my mother's face, it was worth it.

'I take back all the things I've said about her', smiled my mother, her usually pale face glowing, 'she's being so generous now.'

'She's certainly changed', I grinned, 'As everyone knows, she's always been a firm believer in recycling.'

I puffed up the pillows, and straightened Mrs Pogmore's latest gift, a satin-bound blanket, over Mother's thin legs.

'When I get back from Mr Marsh's we'll have a glass of that nice wine Mrs P. gave us.'

And I left for my evening job.

Next day as I eavesdropped from behind a pile of baked bean cans in the village shop, I overheard Irene Wills.

'I knew Mrs Pogmore was going earlier than originally planned,' she told her customer, 'she always confided in me you know.'

'Being pampered in a posh hotel before going on her husband-hunting cruise.' Sniffed Ada Green from behind the Post Office counter.

My final day arrived. I looked around the empty house and as I stood at the foot of the stairs I heard a sound. Had I been a fanciful sort of person I could have believed it was the chuckle of the late Mr Pogmore. But that was nonsense. It was just the sound of a house settling for the night. I stepped out into the evening air and gratefully turned the key. It seemed silly to lock the door on a property that was to be demolished next week, but I like to do things properly. I slipped the key into the pre-addressed envelope to put through the Solicitor's letterbox on my way home.

I rubbed my aching back. The last three weeks had been hard work, transporting recycled gifts, the clearing up and the chopping and slicing. I took my final look round at the once fruitful land; soon this area would be changed for ever. But so would my life. And I need never come this way again. As I mounted my bike, across the valley I saw the lights of Mr Marsh's van as he set out to collect the pig.

One more task before I freewheeled down the hill.

'Here y'are Pig. Last Supper!'

As I cycled past the sty, I chucked the greedy animal the last parcel of sliced and chopped Pogmore. I'm a firm believer in recycling.

Veronica Allerston

NEW START

Post my divorce I had decided to start again, somewhere new where nobody knew me, or my history and I could literally reset the clock and go out on my own. Twelve stone of dead weight gone, and children grown up it was now my time. I was aware that a change of this magnitude, according to my friends, was sheer lunacy but I was determined – basically I had nothing to lose. Even if it was not my forever place it would help me move on in other ways.

I opened out the map of England, got a pin, closed my eyes, turned my hand round a few times and then – struck. When I opened my eyes, I checked where the pin had fallen – Liverpool of all places. Stage one of new life accomplished . I now knew where I was headed. I didn't know anything about Liverpool apart from it being a city - the Beatles came from there, the Cavern where they and many other groups found fame, two major football teams and that was about it. My random selection process meant I would be anonymous to the city, as the city was to me, which at this moment in time was all I asked.

I packed my bags, booked my ticket said my goodbyes and set off. Eastbourne to Victoria, then Euston to Liverpool. Two and a half hours later I arrived at Lime Street Station. The journey was a breeze – and by the time I arrived I was relaxed and ready for anything.

It was now 2 pm so it was a case of best foot forward and first job was to find somewhere to stay. I spotted an amiable looking constable and stopped to ask him for directions. His voice was pure Scouse which was like music to my ears although it was perhaps a touch hard to decipher every word, but I got the gist of his directions.

It was a beautiful day – blue sky, fluffy white clouds – perfect day to start this adventure. Since I had plenty of time, and my case was a pull along one, I set off on foot. It didn't take me long, however, to realise I had misunderstood some of the directions I had been given and was definitely heading the wrong way. I took out my mobile put my glasses on and pulled up a street map put in the road name, post code and the name of the Air BnB. Yep, I was heading in the opposite direction to where I needed to be.

I retraced my steps to the Station and sought out my friendly police constable for help. My mood of enthusiasm and positivity was becoming slightly unsustainable, but I kept going forward with a smile on my face. A quick chat with PC Scouse and I was off again. This time I went through a beautiful park full of people, children playing, dog walkers throwing twigs for their respective pets to fetch. I crossed the bridge over the famous 127 mile long Leeds and Liverpool canal at the other side of the park and there it was – a fantastic building aptly named The Beau Bridge BnB . What a view! Park on one side; canal on the other.

I booked in, put my case in the room and went back outside to enjoy the rest of the day. That's when it happened – my new start in life just took a big hit – there walking along the canal pathway was the cause of my single status and the search for a new life – my ex-husband's lover. We had never met but when I went through the forgive, forget, move on stage, I followed him one night and saw them both in a local restaurant. I knew what she looked like, and I also discovered that stuff forgiveness – it was massively overrated.

I do know, through the grapevine that their relationship failed, as surprise, surprise he turned out to be a serial philanderer, so I decided to approach her and ask her reason for being in Liverpool. I called out to her and she stopped – surprised at being called. I introduced myself by saying 'I think we may have something in common and it's called Dean.' She looked stunned and worried, but I soon put her mind at rest and informed her that it was the best thing that had ever happened to me. Once we got talking - swapping war stories about Dean and his numerous short comings (including his height) we found that we liked one another and as luck would have it, she was staying with friends nearby. More to the point I realised we liked each other. Bonus.

So we, that is Shirley and I, decided to celebrate the loss, if you can call it that - of a twelve stone lummox called Dean and hit the City of Liverpool for a celebratory knees up. Who would have thought it – I come all the way to Liverpool, out of the blue come across my one-time nemesis and we end up making friends. All I can say is Power to the female of the species.

Susan Cooper

A PERFECT PLACE TO HIDE

Tom was silent for a moment then said 'Where's your car, Joe?'

'Got rid of it as soon as possible. Drove it onto the Downs, removed the number plates, poked them into a crack in the ground and covered 'em with rocks. Drove another 5 miles or so to the cliff edge then released the handbrake, set light to it and pushed it over the edge. Flames hit the petrol tank just as it went over. Then cut across the fields 'til I got here.'

Tom relaxed. Having the Police attracted to his place was the last thing he wanted. He thought for a moment then said

'Okay. I can hide you until the furore dies down then we'll decide how to get you away.'

The (dis)honourable Thomas Hardy-Wick had inherited the rambling old house and a considerable amount of land. The grounds to the front of the property he had now turned into a small zoo. Busy in the school holidays and weekends it brought in a reasonable amount of money and was a good cover for Tom's other nefarious activities.

'Let's get some hot food into you then I'll show you where you can stay.'

He pottered around the kitchen tossing bacon and sausages into a pan and baked beans into the microwave and a knife and fork onto the table. Joe sat as though shell-shocked, gazing into space re-living the sound of the impact and the policeman's scream as his legs went under the car.

'Wrap yourself around that, Joe,' said Tom putting the plate in front of him.

The aroma snapped Joe out of his reverie as he realised how hungry he was. Tom slipped into the TV room and watched Joe through the door crack. When Joe pushed his empty plate away Tom called him.

'You'd better come in here, Joe.'

As Joe entered the room Tom snapped off the TV so Joe wouldn't see it wasn't on the News channel.

'Just seen a news flash. Sorry, Mate. The copper is dead, Joe.'

'Oh shit,' responded Joe sinking on to the settee, his head in his hands, 'they're even tougher when it's one of their own. You've got to help me, Tom. Please. Please'

'I said I would.' said Tom placing a hand on his shoulder.

'That's what mates are for. Follow me and I'll show you where I'm hiding you.'

Numbly Joe followed him back into the kitchen. Warm, dry and with a full stomach, the whisky bottle collected en route, Joe followed his friend through a door in the far corner of the kitchen and down the steps into the cellar. At the end of a passage with padlocked doors at intervals, more steps led upwards and through another stout door. Joe found himself inside a small house containing a kitchen-diner, sitting room, bedroom and bathroom. It was quite cosy and reasonably light considering the windows were set so high up.

Joe looked at his grinning friend suddenly realising where he was. This was the little building set in the centre of the lion enclosure. Tom laughed at his friend's horrified face.

'Don't worry mate. It's a perfect place to hide. No one will be brave enough to look for you in here and in the evening when the punters have gone you can come into the main house unless we have other visitors. You'll find your neighbours are a bit noisy but don't worry - they can't get at you as long as you keep the exterior door barred. But it's safe now. And it's stopped raining. C'mon I'll show you.'

He unbarred the door, reluctantly Joe followed him out. It was obvious from what was on the ground that at times the big cats roamed in front of the building but now they were in a cage at the side.

'See?' said Tom, pointing to a glass covered control panel on the outside.

'That operates that grab which Fred, their keeper, loads with meat, lowers it over the cage and drops it in. Greedy devils rush in to feed and then Fred presses the buttons that electronically close the gates. As long as they've got food and access to their sleeping quarters, they're happy overnight. Fred opens them in time for the punters arriving in the morning.'

As he turned to go, he added -

'Oh, there's sort of rent to pay. It'll be your job each evening to go around the enclosure once Fred has caged them up and shovel their shit into sacks. I sell it on to gardening centres. They sell it as cat deterrent. Shit shovelling is the only job Fred doesn't like doing so he'll keep his gob shut about you being here.'

Still grinning, he left. Joe quickly barricaded the door. He slipped between the sheets and lay there anxiously listening to the roar of the lions outside. Then anaesthetised by the remainder of the bottle of whisky he fell into a deep sleep.

Next morning he climbed on a chair to peep out of the window to see a lion and lioness called Sultan and Sheba walk past the sill without even glancing his way.

'Probably doesn't even know I'm here', he thought trying to reassure himself. Most of his day was spent watching the TV and he tried not to think of the dramas of the previous day. Late that afternoon when Fred had gone off duty, Tom showed him where the shovels and sacks were kept. Keeping a cautious eye on the cage where the lions were locked up Joe began to relax.

Days drifted into weeks; Joe was feeling very bored. He'd even started watching CBeebies on TV. Although the hours seemed endless, he was very busy at the start and end of each day; his duties were increasing. After the zoo was closed, he seemed to be turning into keeper's dogsbody, chopping up fruit and vegetables for various animals, preparing the dishes for the morning.

Then before the punters arrived, he was expected to collect them and scour out the mess left behind when the animals had finished. This meant entering their cages.

The zebras seemed to poo more than they ate. He hated the monkeys with their endless chatter, screaming and prancing but hated the parakeets even more as they just let their mess go as they flew, much of it landing on his head and shoulders.

He'd never been particularly keen on animals and now his disgust increased but when he thought of the alternatives to this new situation, he accepted there was no choice.

To add to his boredom Tom held endless parties which meant Joe spent more and more time on his own in the evenings. Many of Tom's guests seemed to have been imported from the local brothel with a lot of noisy goings-on into the early hours. Joe complained about it to his friend and confessed he was worried about his girlfriend Sandra. Had she by now found somebody?

A day later Tom came to him with a big smile on his face and a surprise. The surprise came in the shape of Sandra. Short tight dress with a low-cut neckline, tattooed butterflies trying to escape from her cleavage and very high heels. She and Joe fell into each other's arms and as Tom beat a discreet retreat the dress didn't stay on for long Afterwards Sandra said,

'It's been a long wait. When Tom came to me the day after the incident, I was so relieved you were safe and with him, but I thought he would have brought me to you before now.'

Joe flew into a rage.

'All this time and he's made us both wait! I see his game now; he's kept me here as an unpaid extra zookeeper. '

'Calm down Joe,' she pleaded anxiously, 'where else can you go?'

Outside a lion roared and she clutched at him.

'Hell, Joe, what's that?'

'Just my neighbours.' laughed Joe, relaxing a little.

'Don't worry you are safe with me. They are just a couple of pussycats!'

By the morning, she had adjusted to the strange mooing, crowing, screeching, and trumpeting that emanated from the zoo, and reluctantly they said goodbye, Sandra promising to return as soon as Tom made it possible. Joe's resentment towards his former friend did not abate however but he kept it to himself knowing he was so dependent on him.

Joe had never asked Tom what the corridor cupboards contained as there was a certain honour between rogues. But he now felt that Tom had broken that code, and all was permitted. Waiting until Tom was away from home Joe took out his most treasured possession, his skeleton keys. He systematically worked his way along the corridor opening each door in turn. Most cupboards held the usual domestic junk until he came across one containing two large suitcases. These he also opened. The first was full of jewellery some of which he recognised as having been on Crimewatch as stolen property. The second case was full of bundles of notes. Joe quietly relocked the cases and returned to his little house to think.

He turned on the television and, on the news, the usual Brexit arguments were going on. He paid little attention until the second item of news made him sit bolt upright. A man on crutches was coming slowly down the steps of a building. The announcement was 'Hero policeman discharged from hospital.'

Joe was enraged. All this time Tom had allowed him to think he was a cop killer. Angrily he paced the floor as much a caged animal as the others in the zoo, until gradually his rage subsided to be replaced with icy cold thoughts of revenge.

'Slowly, slowly catchee monkey,' he thought as he cleared the monkeys mess next day, a plan forming in his mind. 'Must let Tom carry on thinking I'm still his ignorant friend until I'm ready to put it into action.'

On Sandra's next visit he told her what he had found. Sandra was shocked and Joe explained his plan for them and a new life. Sandra capitulated immediately. Tom seemed to be holding more parties. Joe was becoming more frustrated at the lack of opportunity to realise the plan. Then eventually Tom announced he was going away on his yacht for three weeks. Joe found it hard to hide his joy but simply said he'd miss him and looked forward to having more time with Sandra instead.

Finally, Tom packed his bags into his limo and said goodbye. He couldn't have chosen a more fortuitous day from Joe's point of view - the day of the Big Match. He sent a text to Sandra with two words; 'it's GO!'

Sandra arrived late that afternoon carrying two bulky travel bags. Joe helped her carry them past the two guards playing cards and although they hardly glanced at them.

'Blimey Girl, what you got in here? Thought you said the conference was only two days?' said Joe.

'Got the files I need for my Presentation,' replied Sandra.

In Joe's room they opened the bags filled with blown up balloons to make them appear bulky. Joe and Sandra giggled as they popped them all. Joe stood on a chair to peep out of the window. He watched the two guards hurry towards Fred's quarters to join the other keepers watching the match on Fred's big screen TV. Then while Sandra stood guard, Joe filled the bags with as much of the cash from the hidden suitcase as their zips would allow. He helped Sandra carry the bags and install them in the boot of her car managing to look dejected enough to fool the gatekeeper into thinking Sandra would be gone for some time. Not that he cared, having made sure the last of the punters had exited, the gatekeeper rushed his locking up, forgetting his usual checking, and hurried off to join his mates.

Joe looked at the clock, time to go poop scooping for the last time. As soon as it became dusk, he would slip away and jog the quarter of a mile to the lay-by where Sandra would be waiting with the money and their passports. By the morning when the gatekeeper found the gate unpadlocked and Joe gone, the two would be on the ferry to the continent and not be seen again. He picked up the shovel and the bags and stepped outside. He turned the corner and was confronted by Sultan and Sheba uncaged and unfed. Empty mouths open, canines sparkling in the failing sunlight. Joe had just a moment to realise his neighbours were not friendly after all.

Veronica Allerston

THE LAST TELEPHONE BOX IN LONDON

The smell in the last phone box was repugnant, but Jack pulled the door shut behind him and started reading the cards pasted to the back wall. The traditional red box had recently gained notoriety, being the last working phone box in London, after a campaign by locals to force the telephone company to keep it and maintain the line. The resulting social media campaign was the cause of the queue that Jack had reached the front of, after a four hour wait. George, the landlord of the Kings Head had been very vague, over lunch, about the special nature of this telephone box but stressed that it was always worth the wait. He had muttered about time travel and local history but then George did seem a bit flaky.

Jack scanned the cards, grubby and faded, sexual services and cab companies were the pattern, but none stood out as different. There were no instructions in the box as to what you are supposed to do once you managed to get in there. The cards blurred into meaningless colours and numbers so Jack looked out of the small windows at the London around him.

The queue was getting impatient outside the box, but one shabby woman kept laughing to herself, in between looking over at George, standing shotgun in the doorway of his pub smoking a lonely cigarette. It was dusk, the pavements were crowded with kids, late home from school, and workers trying to get ahead of the rush hour. The road was slow with traffic, brightly coloured sleek modern vehicles crawling past: cars, buses, taxis, and commercial vehicles. Drivers blowing vape fumes out of the window while ranting into invisible microphones. A nasty child stood on the path spitting into the kerb.

The way the world was changing was kind of musical, Jack felt, when he noticed the headlights go down on the cars and windows and doors darkening in the shops and businesses along the street. He felt like he was sitting in the audience of a theatre just before curtain-up, when the stage lights draw eyes towards the performance. Jack looked over to the Kings Head and noticed the sign, that pompous old Henry VIII, start swinging in a new breeze. Now a wind was getting up, also bringing smoke along the street from some red lights in the distance. It was like the city had caught fire and the sky was catching the colour and holding it up. George had gone from his smoking doorway, his meagre cigarette embarrassed maybe, by the real fire filling the whole sky with toxic clouds.

The phone box queue had dispersed, all souls gone apart from that woman, she was now desperate looking, silent apart from her hands jingling coins in her pockets. She saw Jack looking and banged on the door with her fist, entreating him to exit the box or even open up and let her share. Jack turned his back and pressed it against the door to keep her out. This was when the world outside the box started really changing. Schoolkids were fewer and adults pacing along the path seemed older, dressed in dark hues and beige fabrics, trilby hats on men, and women in practical raincoats. None of the people faltered in the new darkness or blinked at the smoke in the air or appeared to struggle to see in the blackness. Vehicles in the street were suddenly aged, like a wartime matchbox collection, sized up, and noisy engines filled the streets with lead and old petrol smells. Air raid sirens pierced the cacophony of what was now clearly wartime London.

With growing horror Jack remembered the dark history, his son had just learned at school, of 43,500 civilians killed during the aerial bombardment of cities across the country, during the Blitz. Jack saw the people, a steady stream magnified by the air raid sirens calling more and more people to come out of their houses, shops, and workplaces to get to the shelters and underground as fast as possible. They were calm but pushing on, determined to get to safety. How many of these people would survive?

Jack pulled his back away from the phone box door, turned, and pulled it towards him. The door was stuck tight, the stupid woman was pushing in, and he was pulling but it still wouldn't budge. He stopped and banged his fist against the glass on the side of the box. Jack felt like a soldier in a battle, but the only one in the fight who knew this hell wasn't going to be forever and, in fact, just over eight months longer. He knew that battles would rage overhead as brave pilots defended the city, and the country, and would prevail. The War would be won. Of the individuals and around him, some would perish while others survived. London would rise again. The telephone box that enclosed him now would stand strong and remain an icon of the times, a symbol of strength and survival.

It didn't matter what he knew or even what he could see happening here. The people couldn't see him. They couldn't hear anything other than sirens, bombs now falling, exploding all around. They could look up and see searchlights above, highlighting bombers, flack and barrage balloons. The King's Head was on fire in the roof but the sign still hanging from its frame had stopped swinging. There was no more breeze.

In desperation Jack turned again to the cards pasted on the back wall of the phone box. Nothing about their names and numbers made sense. Maybe he had misunderstood George's guidance on how to time travel in this box. Perhaps the telephone box, a solid piece of living history in this part of London, was really the safe place to stay rooted in the present. He only had to distract himself from the madness of old London surrounding him and get to reality.

Jack shovelled some coins into the slot and picked up the handset. He dialled the number on the card George had handed him but was not surprised to see him walk out of the door and light another cigarette. Jack put the phone down. Looking straight into the heart of the phone box George smiled and exhaled slowly.

Jack pulled at the door of the box, and finally it opened. He walked outside. The crazy woman laughed like a Hyena and replaced him in the box. Jack realised he hadn't collected his change but never mind. The world around him looked like 21st Century again, everything lit brighter and moving faster. There were no more bombs or fires.

He decided to make that walk to the Underground, slowly and safely, in his privileged modern world, remembering those who perished, and take a train to another part of London where the streets were less troubled by lost souls. Jack felt a vibration in his breast jacket pocket, and it touched his heart. He reached in and felt the comforting warmth of his smartphone. Maybe carrying his life around on his person wasn't so bad after all.

He took one last glance back before turning the corner. George was out smoking again and the queue at the telephone box was growing.

Wendy Ogden

THE POLICEMAN

The black Audi roared to a halt; the loud music suddenly stopped. A large heavyset man jumped out. He walked up to the front door and banged on it. The door was opened by a slim attractive woman carrying a two-year-old child.

'Here's daddy darling, he's going to take you for a lovely walk in the park, mummy will see you soon. Carl, I'll meet you on the seafront near the Punch and Judy tent. Here's his bag and buggy, I'll see you about three thirty. Don't forget to strap him in.'

'Don't tell me how to look after my son.' Carl snapped. The woman flinched instinctively at the outburst. After years of physical and mental abuse she had left her husband and moved back in with her parents. She had planned to see a solicitor that afternoon. Her mother came to the door.

'Is everything ok Sarah?'

'Yes mum, I'll come in soon.' She handed the little boy to her husband. He took the tiny vulnerable child to the car and strapped him in.

'Bye Jamie, Mummy loves you.'
Jamie waved and then was gone. Sarah burst into tears then noticed a neighbour staring. So, she went in.

Carl was a policeman. He loved his job but had recently been suspended for using excessive force whilst arresting a youth. He already had two official warnings on his file, so it didn't look good. Carl pulled up outside the park, he put Jamie in the buggy and went into a shop opposite. He needed a drink. He bought four cans of lager and opened one. He took a couple of gulps and then they headed for the park.

After queuing for an ice cream for Jamie they walked around the lake watching the ducks squabbling. Carl found a bench and sat sipping his lager. He was oblivious to the other parents glancing disapprovingly at him. After pushing Jamie on the swings, they headed back to the car.

He remembered that in his glove compartment was a joint confiscated from a youth. He opened the window, lit the joint, took a deep gasp and headed for the seafront, which was very was busy. The Punch and Judy tent was situated on the Green with lots of families picnicking. Carl got out, dropped the joint stub and they set off. They found a space. Carl got Jamie out of the buggy sat him down then gave him a snack and a drink. He grabbed another lager then laid back on the grass. The show hadn't started yet. Jamie was busy picking daisies and Carl closed his eyes.

He woke with a start. God, he felt strange. He looked around — Jamie was gone.

'Have you seen my little boy?' He asked people around him. They shook their heads. Standing up he thought he saw Jamie. He rushed to the tent — no sign of him. He pulled back the flap. A strange little man was inside.

'Where's my son?' Carl demanded.

'That's the way to do it!' replied the man in a shrill voice.

'What?'

'That's the way to do it!'

Carl grabbed the man,

'Take that stupid thing out of your mouth!'

He forced the man's mouth open - it was empty. Carl suddenly felt faint, the tent was spinning round and round. He collapsed onto the ground. When he woke up, he couldn't move; he felt like he was shrinking and shrinking. He was dressed in an old-fashioned police uniform. He looked out onto the crowd, Sarah and Jamie were sitting together laughing as Mr Punch began raining painful blows on Carl - 'The Policeman' screeching:-

'that's the way to do it, that's the way to do it!'

David Smith

DAN

Dark clouds were gathering over distant hills and fast. Lucy could not believe it was about to rain again. The sun had been shining earlier and the birds sung loudly, bringing music to Lucy's ears.

Dan, the new man in her life, was coming to visit her tomorrow. She just hoped the weather stayed fine. She had so much planned to do that rain would ruin everything.

Lucy and Dan had been corresponding for months now and she'd got to know him really well. But it was time they met. They couldn't sustain a relationship for much longer without actually meeting each other.

She'd seen pictures of him of course, many times. He looked kind, and handsome too. And he was amenable whenever they spoke. He was someone she would like to know better, and he felt the same he said.

Then an anonymous message arrived, which said, 'Just ask him about his wife.' But Dan had already told her that they'd parted some time ago, acrimoniously too. 'Perhaps it was her trying to cause trouble,' he said. 'Jealous that he was happy.'

Lucy couldn't wait to see him, but she still had a lot to do before he arrived tomorrow. She wanted things to be just right. So, she cleaned the house from top to bottom and even placed flickering, bright, lights around tall, leafless twigs that stood in a large pot in the lounge. It really set the mood and looked so pretty. The rain was still holding up, thank God, so Lucy popped out later to buy a bottle wine. Dan liked red he said.

By the end of the day everything was prepared, and she went to bed more content than ever. She was finally going to meet him.

Lucy got up early that morning, she was expecting Dan about mid-day and couldn't be more excited. She dressed herself in all her finery and applied some pretty make-up. Nothing too outrageous or sexy, but fetching she felt. Let's hope Dan thought the same.

She then pulled out two large wine glasses from the cupboard and placed them down by the bottle of red, which was already on the table and she waited. And she waited some more.

But Dan never showed. She should have guessed he'd been playing her. How could he be so cruel? He didn't even ring to say he'd been called away, or anything.

She'd tried his mobile several times and left messages but he didn't reply. That's it no more men. Just when she thought she'd found Mister Right. She'd even told her friends all about him and her family. How embarrassing.

Lucy started to cry. She felt such a fool. When the doorbell rang. It was him at last. He'd obviously been delayed.

Excited to see his darling face and feel his first touch she opened the door quickly. But a man in uniform stood there, looking glum.

'Sorry Madam, I'm Constable Stanley, I think I may have some bad news. Only Dan Walker was involved in a serious accident earlier this morning and died at the scene. Your address was found on the seat next to him in the car. We thought we should tell you as we guessed you might be waiting.'

Lucy started crying again. Dan had never been to her place before and didn't know the way. She remembered he said he'd written her directions down on a piece of paper so he didn't get lost. But he really was now. Devastated, Lucy drowned her sorrows with a bottle of red that night.

Lena Bowling

FORGETFUL

Well, let's face it, I am really quite old. Forgetful they say. But I don't care, I actually quite like it. Some days dear, I do choose to be forgetful; I find it quite useful. I can get out of all kinds of things I don't want to do. It makes me chuckle to myself. I chuckle quite a lot these days.

There is a lot to be said for being old, you know. The odd ache and pain is a bit of a bore, but apart from that I would say it is just great. I've done everything I was supposed to do in my life. All the obligations, got married, raised children etc, but I also did what I wanted once he died, managed to have quite a few lovers, although I keep quiet about that these days. They seem very moral, now don't they dear. Mind you when I can't sleep, I prefer to count boyfriends than count sheep. That amuses me too. I don't always remember their names, but I certainly remember their faces. Not just their faces either.

Time changes when you get a bit senile you know. I can spend hours just looking out at the garden, in a sort of anaesthetised state, just enjoying it. I watched a ladybird yesterday and sang the rhyme to it. Bit morbid really, what's the point in telling it to go home when it hasn't got one anymore and its children are all gone. Ridiculous. My mind wanders you see. I seem to nod off rather a lot. It's nice.

Of course I can please myself now dear. Some days I don't even bother washing and I can never remember if I have had breakfast, so often I can have two or three. I do like cocoa pops. Yes, I suppose I do smell a bit, I just blame the cat. I refuse to open the post, never worry about money, or look at bills, I reckon there isn't much they can do about it at my age. They can hardly put me in prison. Well, I wouldn't really care if they did, save me cooking and I like interesting people.

I don't go out much now since I learned to grocery shop on the thing, amazing. All very easy, lovely delivery boy, bless him, but getting rid of the gin bottles remains a bit tricky. I 've given up on that now and just put them in the wardrobe. That'll do.

The best thing now is remembering when I was young, long before you were born, my dear. I can remember that without any trouble at all. The doctor says my long-term memory is intact. He tries to be kind, but he looks about fourteen and has no idea really. How can he know what it's like to be old? I know what it's like to be young though. He gave me medicine; the chemist delivers it once a month. I don't take it, makes me feel funny and I remember Thalidomide. I could never get the pills out of those foil packages anyway. What was wrong with a glass bottle? I just put it in the bin, saves argument.

Oh yes dear, I remember the old days. I shared a flat in London. My what we girls got up to. It was a riot! Two pairs of false eyelashes and a mini skirt exactly two inches below my bum. And PVC boots! Difficult going upstairs on the bus though. I was a dollybird, can't say that now, of course, they think it's demeaning. I didn't, just loved it. Never paid for drinks or meals, that was up to the boys. It was great being female, saved loads of money. I loved the clothes then, I don't bother so much now, I always manage to drop bits of my dinner down them. There are several genders now, they can choose. A bit confusing I always think.

Well, it's a beautiful afternoon. I think May is the best month. Oh, July is it? Well then, I think I'll strip down to my vest and pants and lie on the grass in the garden and have a little nap. No, don't you worry about the neighbours, nosy lot, I just give them the finger. Been nice talking. Who did you say you were again? Social Worker, oh well that's nice my dear. Don't you go worrying your head about me, never been better!

Jane Kenton-Wright

LIVE AND LET LIVE

Abhorrent! Downright nasty! Susan wanted to laugh. What was wrong with her? She was turning into someone she didn't recognise. It was windy, and the buffeting car was filled with a glorious musical accompaniment, as she drove to her next clients.

Her first visit had involved being subjected to the demented bed bound old woman, her body twisted under the covers, spitting insults at her and shouting and swearing. This had been interspersed with chanting and then times of quiet. During previous times, the woman had engaged in calm and lucid conversation with Susan about the colourful flowers in the garden and beauty of the sea in all weathers. It was hard to predict how things would be from one week to the next.

The woman was cared for by her retired nurse alcoholic daughter who did her best and Susan, similar in age, liked her. Support was also provided by two sisters living locally who also tried to clear up the squalid conditions in the house from time to time. Mother and daughter were imprisoned at home together and the daughter's only escape was when Susan came each week to offer three hours respite.

Back in the car, music stimulating her senses, Susan's expletives were not about the people she had come from but about the elderly man next. Denis cared for his wife, Mary, if you could call it that. Determined to see the best in people, it had taken a while for Susan to realise that he was a complete control freak and a cruel man. He had stripped the dignity away from poor Mary, patronising her, talking about her in horrible personal ways in front of her, making insulting remarks about her appearance and talking about her as if she was invisible.

Mary, diagnosed with mild dementia, had deteriorated little in the two years of Susan's weekly visits. She could still prepare a light meal, see to most of her personal care, mobilise herself slowly, hold a conversation and remember her friends and family. It suited Denis to make out how little she could do to look after herself, and how he couldn't leave her alone, as he could claim every benefit having driven them into debt with his selfish spending. He had also made sure that she was totally dependent on him. Often, he made her insecure, inducing panic attacks when he left the house at times because she didn't know if he would return. Mary had confided in Susan that this insecurity stemmed from when he had taunted her once, earlier in their relationship, when she had threatened to leave, that he would be the one to leave first.

Denis never stopped talking - long boring stories about himself and his life whilst Mary sat quietly staring into space. She had almost become numb - switched herself so that she was untouchable by this asinine, pompous, self-centred man.

Susan had gradually realised all of this and longed for Denis to leave her alone with Mary who came out of herself when he wasn't there. The two women sat side by side on the scruffy sofa, complete with threadbare throw, and chatted happily. This was Mary's time to feel good about herself and recount stories of her life. She had a repertoire of all the things she felt comfortable talking about and could remember – her strict Methodist upbringing, the hardships of having to walk miles in the countryside in all weathers to get to school and church and her young life growing up on a farm. A particularly happy time for her was the freedom of travelling by bus to secondary school and getting out of the confines of the village. There, she could be herself, made lifelong friends and felt more independent and free.

She talked endlessly in details about her uniform - she still even had her old maroon school scarf which was very warm and she would wear on cold days. Her working life had been in a bank which she enjoyed. She was in her late thirties when she married Denis, owning a house which was very unusual or a woman in those days. Denis had changed all that, never allowing her to go out without him apart from to work.

Susan's visits were to provide respite so that the Carer could go out but Denis rarely would. He would disappear for short periods to his workshop where he tinkered with model cars and aeroplanes. Over time, more and more of them came inside, piled high with various books and tools, on the table to the side of his chair. This was another dirty untidy house where there was stuff on every surface and corner in the small bungalow.

On their own, Susan and Mary would relax and giggle together. Susan recounted amusing little stories in parallel to Mary's regular offerings. However, Susan would soon hear the creak of a floorboard in the hall so realising that Denis was hovering and listening. The moment he entered, like a light, Mary would switch off. Week after week, Denis would sit with them in the messy hot sitting room, more dust gathering on the glass TV stand. He would talk about Mary's incontinence, how she didn't wash herself properly, how fat she was, how he had always chosen her clothes as she had no colour sense and recount details of appointments where he dragged her to London for Dementia research. Poor Mary would just sit there but often scowl or glower at him.

When he brought in the tea, hers was in a plastic child's beaker in case of spillage. How humiliating for her as she was more than capable of managing a cup.

As Susan parked outside, she remembered the embarrassing conversation the week before. Mary was having a minor operation soon and Denis, tossing a coin for heads or tails, was confused about the question of a Do Not Resuscitate. He said that he thought the medics were suggesting that as a matter of course, this should be put into place for Mary. Susan had turned to her and asked her more than once if she would like to be resuscitated and

Mary said 'yes, I would. I am not ready to die.' Denis's face had fallen, and a look of pure hatred had crossed Mary's often expressionless face. It was just awful.

Susan slammed the car door shut, braced herself and went down the little path to the front door. Denis had installed a camera doorbell, so she put on her best face and rung it. No answer until eventually, the door was opened by Mary.

'Come in' she said and turned to shuffle the short distance into the sitting room and Susan followed.

'Where's Denis?' she asked.

There was no need for a reply since Susan saw him lying in front of the grate by his chair, a maroon woollen scarf round his neck. Mary sat down on the sofa. 'Do not resuscitate' is all she said.

Caroline Scotter

THE DESERT

Steve picked up a car from the hire office having landed ninety minutes earlier in Los Angeles. He was there for two weeks finalising some details on a new film. Most of it had been done in Pinewood but the producers wanted him there on a few technical details they weren't happy with - very simple glitches - and he didn't mind. A free trip, all expenses paid - great.

They didn't have the car he wanted, something sporty; instead, a SUV family car. Not the image he was trying to project. A big disappointment. He had the weekend off before work on Monday and was glad to be abroad, away from the cold grey skies and the congestion of the London traffic. He didn't care for Los Angeles, but a two-hour drive could take you away from the sprawling city and the transient pleasures it offered, onto empty desert roads where you could drive without traffic lights, or speed cameras; just lots of empty space and big skies. He loved it. But first - get out of the city.

A sudden deluge had slowed everything down on the freeway; six lanes of traffic going nowhere. Eventually the traffic began moving again and he headed in the direction of Las Vegas: five hours away. After three hours, the jet lag was kicking in, so he stopped at a diner, had a black coffee and something to eat, then set off again. He bypassed Vegas heading into the wide empty space beyond. He planned to find a small town and stop at a motel. Seeing the real America now, it was dusk, with a beautiful sunset.

Steve noticed the fuel was getting low, he would fill up at the next gas station. In his rear-view mirror, he noticed a small beat-up truck. One of the headlights was broken so there were two lights on one side, and only one on the other. The flat-bed truck roared past him, horn blasting. Bloody rednecks, thought Steve. Fifteen minutes later he saw the lights of a small gas station. The Redneck was already filling his truck and Steve could see everything in the back. Some timber, a tarpaulin sheet and what looked like rifles in a long box. God, why do they love their rifles so much?

The Redneck finished filling up, glanced at Steve with dead eyes and went in to pay for the fuel. While he was inside, Steve peered into the truck again. Something red was sticking out of the tarp, it was a shoe. Steve leaned forward. Oh my God, the shoe was on a foot. He stared again, yes it was definitely a foot.

The fuel would have to wait. Steve quickly started his car and drove off. In his rear-view mirror he could see Redneck watching him speeding away, then going to the rear of his truck. Steve put his foot down, getting as far away from the gas station as he could. He grabbed his mobile and saw it had no signal. It was dark now, a beautiful desert night, sky full of stars. Steve was focussed on driving as fast as he could, checking the mirror for any sign of a vehicle behind him. He needed to get to a town - any town. The empty road seemed to stretch ahead of him, going on forever.

Suddenly a ping; the fuel warning light had come on. Oh no, nothing around but desert! Half an hour later the car slowed and spluttered to a halt. The fuel gauge was below zero. With rising fear, Steve saw in his mirror a vehicle coming up behind him. Getting closer, two headlights on one side only one on the other.

The flat-bed truck slowed as it passed Steve in his stationery vehicle. It accelerated on and then in the distance brake lights showed Redneck slowing again until the vehicle stopped. What was he going to do? Steve didn't know but he had nowhere to go and nothing to do but sit and wait to find out.

On the other hand, it was a beautiful night, and the scenery *was* spectacular. He was tired of sitting behind the wheel, so he opened the door and stepped out of the car. He leaned against the door. Steve reached into his jacket pocket for his cigarettes, just one left, and the lighter. The air was fresh after the deluge and the sky so clear above him. Steve looked up to the stars, clicked on his lighter and enjoyed his last cigarette.

David Smith

RISING HIGH

Rob, 42, very wealthy and single, was the Architect of his own apartment block, where he occupied the entire penthouse apartment as his London home. Rob was also the architect of his own isolation, as up there in the sky, and with his own purpose designed penthouse lift, he never met any of his neighbours.

Working from home, running his various businesses online, Rob took his breaks up on the roof garden, the one he had designed for this very purpose. He still felt a rush as he surveyed the panoramic view of the city, but sadly had only Stan, a one-eyed seagull to talk to about his problems. Stan was a good listener, his apparent friendship combined with an insatiable hunger for cold sliced ham, wrapped around oil-soaked anchovies. Rob's housekeeper, Annette, prepared the bird food for him, opening the tins of fish and wrapping them individually in ham as Rob could not bear the feel of oil or fish on his hands. Or the smell. Yet still he liked hand feeding the bird.

One Saturday morning in April, Annette was extremely late for work. She was so angry at her ex-boyfriend, who had failed to turn up, give the children breakfast, and take them to school so she could get to work on time. After mopping the kitchen floor, she realised the bird food still needed preparing and rushed the job, cutting herself deeply on the anchovy tin. Her index finger bled profusely over her wet floor, giving her cause to slide right across it, bumping the still full mop bucket and crashing her headfirst into the gigantic American smart fridge. The monster was confused into action, bumping crushed ice out of its chute, and showering her bleeding, bruised body in the wake of the disinfectant wave which carried her there.

Returning from the roof, after a difficult conversation with Stan, who had swooped over Rob's head, digging his angry claws into his scalp each pass, then defecating over his shoulder, the stink of yesterday's anchovies hanging heavy on him, Rob went straight to the laundry room. He stripped and dumped his clothes before getting into the shower. Forgetting he even had a housekeeper, let alone a woman called Annette, he walked naked into the kitchen for a mouthful of coffee, strong enough to wipe the memory of that terrible smell from his nose.

Annette reversed herself away from the fridge and pulled herself to a sitting position in the bloody pool of rapidly melting ice settling around her. Endeavouring to pull herself upright she turned and looked straight into the bare hairy knees of her employer standing in the doorway of the kitchen. Then she looked up. Annette gasped.

Rob realised he had a mountain to climb when he saw the horrified expression on his housekeeper's face, or rather a quick decision to make. First thought was back to the laundry room for a towel or something to cover himself. He could do that before helping the woman up and out of the sticky mess she was practically floating on. It was that or he could just offer her a hand and pull her up off the floor. Unsure if it was cowardly or more considerately, he decided on the former action.

'I'll be back,' he shouted, as he turned his back and vacated the room.

'Oh my God,' Annette said to herself.

'So now you think you're Arnie?' she asked of his retreating bottom.

Returning in his freshly laundered gym kit, Rob helped Annette to a chair, cleaned her cut finger and applied a firm dressing. He applied a bag of frozen peas to her swollen ankle, twisted in the slide, then drove her to the local hospital minor injuries unit. After holding Annette's right hand, while the doctor stitched her left, then taking Annette home, Rob returned to the penthouse to survey the scene. Bloody, stinking of fish, and alive with the chaos of endeavour and indignity, his kitchen now had a sense of humanity about it which had never featured in his original plans. Now he knew who his housekeeper was, Annette, and even where she lived, a ground floor flat on a disreputable estate, for the first time in his life Rob felt a little more grounded.

Still, Rob needed to get back up onto the roof and chuck a few slices of ham to Stan. This relationship with the bird was one he had started, and he felt some responsibility towards him. Plus, Stan had been perched on the outside kitchen windowsill beak-tapping away, oblivious, or uncaring about the chaos inside. Rob also had quite a lot to share with his feathered friend. He talked about Annette, and where she lived, and the broken-up car on her neighbour's front lawn. How they had sat in her front porch and drank builders' tea while she explained the rules of the ball game, Kerby, her kids were playing across the street. A couple of cars came along but they all stopped, waiting for the throw, respecting the game. He told Stan about the supermarket shopping trolley outside her door, and kids flying up and down the pavements on little scooters with smaller ones pedalling along in miniature plastic cars. Two women were arguing about a debt while another two nattered over rose pruning. An elderly man mowed his lawn, the noise competing with some rap music blasting out of a nearby bedroom window. The whole place felt so alive and even smelled of mince. Rob quite fancied some plain old mince. Stan, good listener as ever, devoured the ham.

    Afterwards Rob mopped the floor and cleaned all the surfaces, Stan was going to have to be more flexible, he decided, while he addressed his own housekeeping for the rest of the week. At least. Shouldn't be so hard, he thought as he looked around his luxury kitchen in the sky. He remembered his original plans and drawings and while he unpacked his grocery delivery, previously ordered by Annette, he thought about shopping trolleys, social housing, low-rise buildings, and trees and kids playing out and hungry birds all over the place.

Wendy Ogden

The Scribe Tribe are :-
- Veronica Allerston
- Lena Bowling
- Tina Burnett-Evans
- Susan Cooper
- Jackie Harvey
- Jane Kenton-Wright
- Gladys Lopato
- Denis MacReever
- Wendy Ogden
- Caroline Scotter
- David Smith
- Beryl Teso

Printed in Great Britain
by Amazon